AUNT BIRDIE AND OTHER STORIES

THOMAS H. OGDEN

Advance Praise for *Aunt Birdie and Other Stories*

It is a wondrous mystery to read the stories of Thomas Ogden. He creates living characters out of the air. Each becomes utterly real to me, and I feel I have always known them. Maybe they resemble people I have encountered briefly or cared for, or perhaps they embody hidden aspects of myself. Regardless, I care deeply about their fates, and I learn from their unpredictable journeys.

—Matthew Zapruder, author of *I Love Hearing Your Dreams*
and *Story of a Poem*

For me, the great joy of reading Ogden begins with the company of Ogden's pellucid mind and vast compassionate heart — of listening in while a master explores the craft of listening itself, the art of hearing and feeling with infinite attunement. But the pleasure of reading Ogden soars, like that of all fine literature, on pure storytelling. From the first page to the last, in this marvelous new collection, I felt swept forward as if in a dream not unlike life — mysteriously compelling and always unmistakably true. Odgen's characters, including husbands and wives and a girl who lives in language, are deeply familiar, as are the questions haunting them all: Who are we, really, to one another? By what laws of chemistry do certain feelings germinate across decades before blossoming into light?

—Daniel Duane, author of *A Mouth Like Yours, A Novel*
(Farrar, Straus & Giroux).

In his latest work of fiction, Aunt Birdie and Other Stories, Thomas Ogden creates an array of fragile yet strong characters. With unflinching honesty and keen perception, Ogden's stories are tinged with the regret, hope, loss, and self-doubt of people reflecting on the past as they strive to do the best they can in the present. Steeped in wisdom, and with a touch of nostalgia, Aunt Birdie and Other Stories is a thoughtful collection boldly told.

—Diane Lechleitner, author of *Faron Goss*,
Gold Winner Foreword Indies Fiction

Other Books by Thomas H. Ogden

Fiction

The Parts Left Out: A Novel

The Hands of Gravity and Chance: A Novel

This Will Do … : A Novel

Non-Fiction

Projective Identification and Psychotherapeutic Technique

The Matrix of the Mind: Object Relations and the Psychoanalytic Dialogue

The Primitive Edge of Experience

Subjects of Analysis

Reverie and Interpretation: Sensing Something Human

Conversations at the Frontier of Dreaming

This Art of Psychoanalysis: Dreaming Undreamt Dreams and Interrupted Cries

Rediscovering Psychoanalysis: Thinking and Dreaming, Learning and Forgetting

On Not Being Able to Dream: Selected Essays, 1994-2005 (available only in Hebrew)

Creative Readings: Essays on Seminal Analytic Works

The Analyst's Ear and the Critic's Eye: Rethinking Psychoanalysis and Literature (co-authored with Benjamin Ogden)

Reclaiming Unlived Life: Experiences in Psychoanalysis

Coming to Life in the Consulting Room: Toward a New Analytic Sensibility

What Alive Means: Psychoanalytic Explorations

AUNT BIRDIE AND OTHER STORIES

THOMAS H. OGDEN

ISBN (perfect): 978-19159-524-8-6
ISBN (hardcover): 978-19159-524-9-3
ISBN (epub): 978-19159-525-0-9

"A Morning with Maria Kodama" is based on an essay originally published in Fort Da 30:17-27, 2024.

First printed September, 2025
by Sphinx (an imprint of Sul Books, LTD)
Lewes, UK / Rodenbourg, LUX
Cover Image: Woman in Window by Sandra Ogden
Interior and Cover Design: Sul Books

Find our books at SULBOOKS.COM

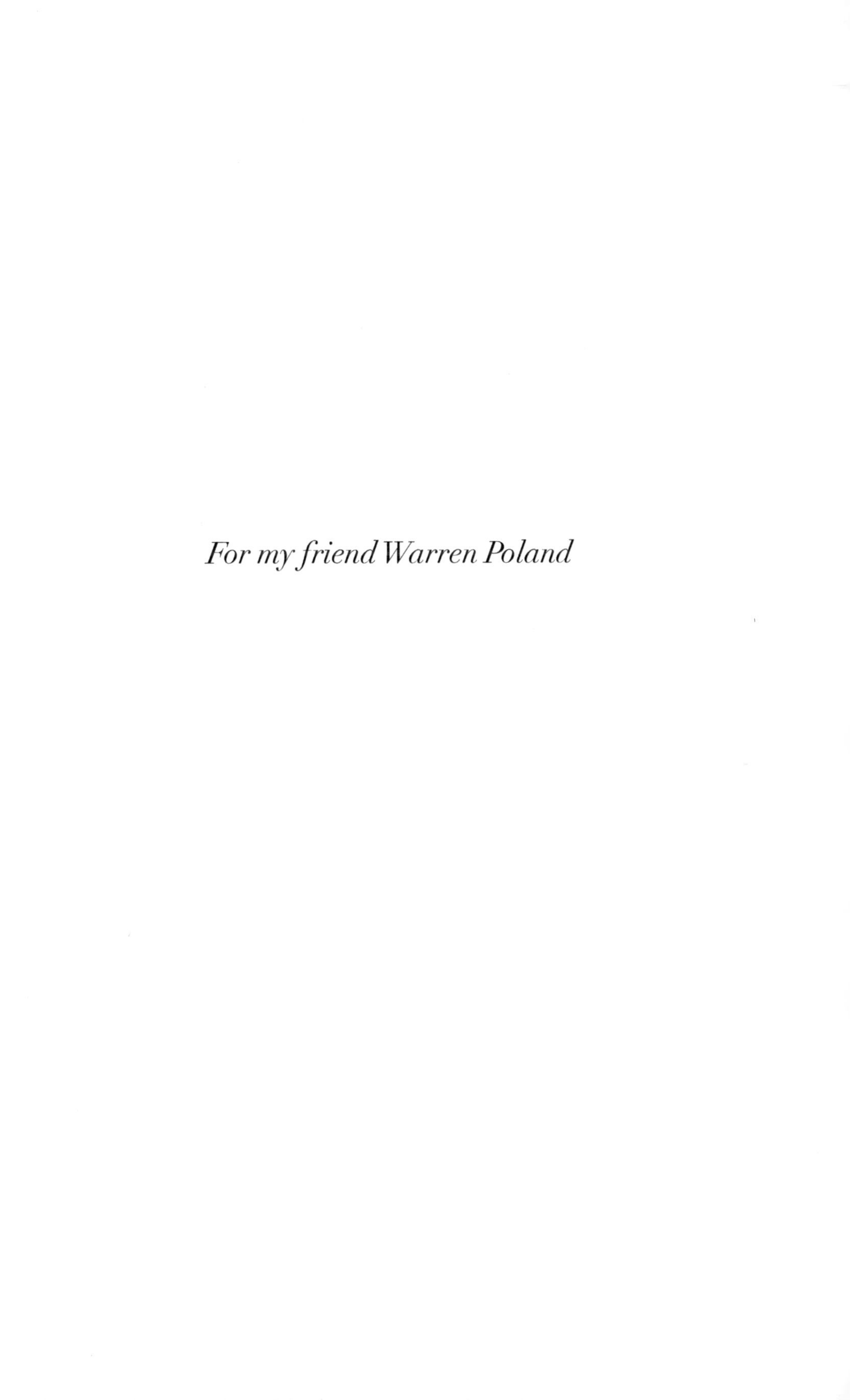

For my friend Warren Poland

WITHIN

— Introduction —

In the past, I have been asked how I go about writing fiction and have not been able to offer a response that has satisfied me. The mythic idea of the Muses has never rung true to me because neither my ideas nor my style of writing feels as if it comes from a source that visits me, that is external to me. The people I have known and the life I have lived are the sources I draw upon and that draw upon me as I write.

Looking back now as I complete this collection of stories, I find I am better able to put into words my experience of writing fiction.

I begin with a rough idea about the sort of situation I would like to create in the piece I am writing, a situation I find intriguing, disturbing, or interestingly complex. For example, a situation in which a woman returns a child she has adopted; in which a man accidentally kills his wife; in which a man marries his half-sister; in which a man secretly has two families. These situations may be derived from events in my own life, from a friend's life, or from events I have read or heard about — or even situations that just come to mind.

I then turn to the work of inhabiting the situation I'm imagining with characters who feel real to me. Of course, the person I know best is myself. I have changed in the course of my life, so I am many people upon whom I can draw. There are also many other people to draw upon: people I've known or heard about, characters in books, and people in newspaper articles I've read. I use one person or combine people as I begin to define the character. I have in my mind a history for each character, which I may or may not elaborate on in the text. I then "introduce" the characters to one another as I experiment (as I write) with ways they might relate to one another. For example, they may draw out, complement, inspire, antagonize, dominate, or submit to another character. The situation I begin with changes, and acquires depth as the characters interact with one another as I write. I do most of this work in the act of writing, not by working things out in my mind and then writing them down.

Unless I am surprised by what I'm writing, the writing is lifeless. When I am writing well, I have the feeling that I couldn't have predicted what is happening. This applies as much to the writing itself (the writing style) as to the development of the characters and the storyline.

As I write, the experience must feel spontaneous, without design. Only in that way am I able to bring to the page more than I know, and only by writing spontaneously do the lines become layered and convey multiple meanings. If the lines can only be read in one way, the story feels uninteresting to me. In my own life, I do not know anything for certain. Everything exists in an atmosphere of "could be," "may be," "probably," and "unlikely." This must also be true in the stories I write. The characters must live in the realm of mystery and uncertainty.

I write fiction by creating scenes. The scenes are comprised largely of events organized around conversations between characters, although, occasionally, a character is thinking about his life and the situation in which he finds himself. As I write, the characters acquire voices as they speak to one another or to themselves. In writing, there are no actors. The voice created in the writing defines the character. If the voices of two characters are undifferentiable, I have not created two distinct characters.

As a scene acquires a measure of solidity, I experiment with adding a scene prior — or subsequent — to it. This stage, in which I am extending the sequence of scenes forward and backward, requires a good deal of time. What I am doing at this point is pushing the limits of what I feel a character is capable of being and capable of doing. As I press a character toward his limits, the character must remain real to me (he must not become larger than life). People behave in ways that are remarkable, unusual, and improbable; in fiction, the remarkable, the unusual, and the improbable must also be plausible. Characters are interesting to the extent that they surprise me (and themselves), but the characters must remain human.

As the sequence of scenes begins to integrate into a storyline, I begin to attend to the craft of writing: word choice; structure of sentences; use of first-, second-, or third-person narration; use of metaphor; narrating in present or past tense; structure of dialogue; use of dialect, and so on. The trick is not to let the craft ("the carpentry") kill the art.

At this stage, I find that the most effective way to improve the writing is to sculpt: to create not by adding, but by paring away. I remove everything that does not contribute to the action of the piece. Extra words make reading the text feel tiring to me. Each time I read the story, I delete more, until I reach a point where I am no longer sure whether a deletion makes the text stronger or weaker. Then I stop.

In this volume, the first six chapters are fictional stories, while the final one, "A Morning with Maria Kodama," is a nonfiction story.

— Aunt Birdie —

When my father died, I inherited Birdie Berliner, whom I knew as Aunt Birdie, though she was my father's aunt, not mine. He and I visited her apartment from the time I was two or three years old, maybe younger, when the visits began. She lived on the Upper West Side in an apartment in a three-story building with a café on the ground floor. I remember her apartment on the top floor as large and bright: a living room with windows on two sides, I think there were two bedrooms. The kitchen was small. Pigeons perched, left droppings, and made croaking sounds on the ledge outside the large double-hung windows. She always seemed ancient to me, though as I think about it now, she was only in her 40s when we first visited her. She seemed to grow younger as I grew older. I remember being told that her husband, Uncle Arthur, was very busy and traveled much of the time in connection with his work. He was there occasionally when we visited. I don't remember much about him other than that he seemed much older than Aunt Birdie.

What I remember most clearly from those visits to Aunt Birdie's apartment was her being very patient with me as she showed me parts of her stamp collection each time we visited. I'm told that Aunt Birdie and I, when I was very young, made outings to the Natural History Museum, the Planetarium, and the Empire State Building. We'd go to Shraft's for ice cream afterward. I have only a fragmentary memory of this.

My father would mention her to me now and again. He loved her as much as he loved my mother, I thought. He told me she was as much of a mother to him as was his own, who I'm told was bedridden with a mysterious illness much of her life.

Despite my father's urging, I stopped going with him on his Sunday visits to Aunt Birdie when I was twelve or thirteen. I was preoccupied with my own troubles at that time. During those years, my life felt unreal to me, a successful semblance of what other people had in mind for me.

I saw Aunt Birdie again at my father's funeral at Temple Emanuel. I was 34. She was small and frail, her jewelry and clothes were from a different era. We spoke briefly, after which she disappeared from the funeral gathering.

A year or so after my father's death, I received a call from Aunt Birdie's doctor in New York saying that she had fallen and broken her hip. She had mentioned me to him and had given him my phone number as someone to call if the need arose. He said he thought she was lonely and could use any help I could give her when she was released from rehab. Given the fact that I lived on the opposite coast, it wasn't clear to me how much help I could be. I told him I'd be glad to be of what help I could, already feeling burdened by this intrusion.

When I called Aunt Birdie at her room in the rehab hospital, she was surprised to hear my voice. She spoke with a Manhattan accent with its sharp nasal tones. It was kind of me to phone, she said. She fumbled for a polite way of asking me how I'd heard that she'd fallen and how I'd found her phone number at the rehab center. I told her that Dr. Nathans had called me. She apologized for his forcing himself and her upon me. She said she hadn't given him permission to call me. I tried to assure her that I was glad to have received the call and wanted to help her with her return to her apartment. She would have nothing of it, insisting that she didn't need help, but sounded genuinely pleased that I had called. My father would have taken the next plane from wherever he was to accompany her back to her apartment. I felt guilty for doing less. We talked about things that she'd been doing while in rehab: reading Philip Roth's new novel and writing letters to her Senator, Hillary Clinton, about the terrible treatment of the soldiers back from Iraq. She was surprisingly animated and seemed to mistake me for my father in a way that created a smooth shift of trust and affection from him to me. I was touched by that transfer of love, but was reluctant to accept it, for I knew that it came with responsibilities. She interrupted herself several times to apologize for taking up my time.

I asked Aunt Birdie how Arthur was. Her voice broke as she told me that things between her and Arthur were difficult. She reminded me that he had been a professor of Physics and Dean of the Faculty at NYU. When he retired, he continued to serve as a visiting professor at universities and research institutions. Until recently, these visits had lasted only six or eight weeks. But last month he accepted a year-long post in Europe and did not invite her to come with him. He acted as if this was an agreement the two of them had always had. I asked if she took this to be his way of saying that he was separating from her in preparation for a divorce. She said she didn't know, that was unclear, but he was very full of himself and highly sensitive to indications that his stature in academia was waning.

Aunt Birdie said she's an old lady with old lady problems and I should not be burdened with her.

I called her on Sundays as I had called my parents when they were alive. She seemed to be waiting for my calls and had something she wanted to say each time. "I may be telling you more than you want to know, so I would be grateful to you if you would tell me." She told me that her parents were people who lived in a late-19th-century time warp. Everything was done in the proper way in their house on the outskirts of Boston. Her schoolteachers were invited to afternoon tea; she took piano and horseback riding lessons; she dutifully studied after dinner and went to bed at 9:00.

During her high school years, her parents entertained the rabbi from their synagogue, a man in his late 40s. Aunt Birdie told me she had a surreptitious romance with this man, which included their sleeping together during the time she was supposed to be taking Bible study lessons from him. She said that I was probably shocked that she was telling me about her romantic life. I told her the truth: I was honored that she trusted me sufficiently to entrust me with confidences. She continued. Her parents encouraged the friendship with the rabbi. She said that the word "ironic" always brought this romance to mind. She was too young for this relationship with a man almost 30 years her senior, but she did not object to it — she genuinely took pleasure in it — because she felt that the only thing about her that held value to anyone was the fact that she was very pretty. "It will be hard for you to imagine that I was once pretty."

Aunt Birdie told me that she was an Assistant Professor of Medicine at NYU when she met Arthur who was teaching in the Physics Department.

"I came down with TB a couple of years after Arthur and I married and was confined to my bed for months at a time. We entertained by moving my bed into our living room where our bohemian friends gathered. Arthur could not have been a more loving husband. We drank too much. People drank more in those days. At about the same time, I developed an intense compelling need to get some things 'right' in my mind before I could turn the door-knob of the door between one room and the next in our apartment on West 10th. For years I would have to get *just right* in my mind the taste of a Martini that Arthur and I drank at our favorite restaurant in the Village many years earlier. When I was able to get it just right, it was like having a release comparable to an orgasm. I hope I'm not embarrassing you. I suppose you'll manage. You're not the little boy who came to visit me with your father. You were a very cute little boy. I suppose I was all right at behaving "just like" a mother, but I would have been hopeless at being a mother. My not having children didn't feel like a choice that I was making, though I suppose it was. There just didn't seem time for it."

"Do you wish you had had children?" I asked, hoping she would say she did.

"Between battling TB and the academic careers Arthur and I were living, there was so much to do — so much I wanted to do — that the matter of having children just never presented itself. You must remember that a woman in academic medicine was a rarity at the time. And before I knew it, it was too late."

After a few moments of silence, Birdie said, "It would be lovely to be surrounded by children and grandchildren. But if I'm honest with myself, that seems like a terrible bother, too. I'm not the motherly sort."

"That's not true. You and I had good outings together."

"Yes, we did. We were already living up here on the Upper West Side when you and your father came to visit. I liked you. Actually, I loved you. I still do. But you were easy to love because I didn't have to take care of you. We had our excursions. You loved the Hayden Planetarium and the ice cream we'd get at Shrafts on 42nd Street. I so enjoyed our outings, and you. It's getting late. I'll let you go. Talk soon." Click.

When I called a few days later, Aunt Birdie said in an animated voice, "Oh, Leonard, there's something I left out when I talked with you last Sunday. I wanted to tell you that after being treated for TB, I returned full-time to academic medicine. Arthur and I began drinking heavily. We were both alcoholics for quite a number of years. I don't want to think how many. This sounds terrible but our careers flourished during that time. We both published a great many journal articles, and I was promoted to Associate Professor of Medicine. That's when Arthur gained a great deal of attention for his research work on cold fusion. I must be terribly boring going on about myself this way. Why would any of this be of interest to you?"

"You'll have to take it on faith that I am interested in what you're telling me."

Aunt Birdie's stories moved easily from one event to another as if she had waited all her life to tell her stories to someone. I occasionally made a statement of surprise or understanding, but I knew I was only meant to listen.

With Arthur away on his one-year visiting professorship in Bonn, Aunt Birdie was housebound unless one of her two friends, Julia and Cecily, accompanied her to a doctor's appointment, or to shop, or occasionally to see a movie or a play. One day Birdie told me about Nell, their housekeeper. "She is a principal personage — not even a person really — in my life. I do not dare say anything to anybody about the fact that Nell is hiding things from me, and stealing some things as well, because people will think I'm a crazy old lady. She hides things that are important to me like a purse my mother gave me or a candelabra that has been in my family for generations. Nell hides these things, and I can tell she takes pleasure in my asking her if she's seen them, so she can tell me she hasn't, and that she'd noticed them missing and had thought I'd moved them. They appear weeks, or sometimes months, later, in places in the apartment where I've checked many times before. Or they don't reappear at all. If I were to tell anyone about this, they would think I'm being absent-minded, or more likely, demented. They'd think that there is no reason in the world why Nell would want to torment me. She's been with us for more than twenty years. When it began a couple of years ago, I couldn't imagine why she would behave like that."

A week later, Birdie told me that Arthur had emailed her saying that the funding for his visiting professorship had been cut off and that he'd be returning home in a month or so. "I don't know how to respond. I don't think I want to live in our apartment with him again. I quite like living alone. I wrote to him yesterday saying I hadn't decided whether he was welcome to live here any longer. I don't think you can understand how bold it was of me to tell him he may not be welcome in the apartment that we've shared for more than forty years.

"He responded almost immediately — as they say in books, 'with dispatch' — that he hoped we could talk about this when he returned. I replied saying that I'd think about it."

Aunt Birdie became preoccupied by the idea that Nell was attempting to drive her mad. She surmised that Nell was doing this out of jealousy of the "opulent" life she and Arthur had, though from Birdie's perspective, that opulence consisted only of their having a large apartment in a nice section of the city, though they paid very little in rent because the apartment was rent-controlled.

Some weeks later, Birdie told me, "Since his return, Arthur has behaved himself and has spoken to me in a more respectful way than he's done in a long time. This week we enjoyed one of our favorite ways of spending time with one another. He read to me from *The Voyage of the Beagle*. His reading to me is something we've done almost all our lives together, though it has become far less frequent during recent years. I don't know how long this change is going to last. He can be like this for periods of time. I'm getting tired. Would you excuse me?" Click.

Nell became more and more difficult for Birdie to handle. She told Arthur she'd like to let Nell go, but he said that there was nothing to tie Nell to the disappearances of things, so he didn't know how to tell her why she was being fired. Birdie felt that Arthur was placing his own convenience above the fact that she no longer felt at home in her own apartment.

One day I received a phone call from Birdie telling me she'd had a fall as she got out of the bath and injured the same hip again. It wasn't a fracture, just a bone contusion. It would heal, but she'd never felt more desolate in her life. She said she was in a great deal of pain and could not talk for very long. A few days later, when I called, Birdie told me that the pain in her hip had persisted, so she was in bed most of the time. She said she didn't know how she could maintain her sanity.

During a call a week or two later, Birdie told me that there was something she had not told me, and in fact, had never told anyone. She didn't know why she felt a need to tell me, but during her residency, she was very lonely and had slept with four of the other medical residents. This was something she felt deeply ashamed of. I understood she was not telling me about these events in hopes I'd give her forgiveness. She just needed to feel less alone with what she was telling me.

When she told Arthur about her having slept with a number of fellow residents, she expected he'd feel shocked and repelled even if he didn't show it. What he said, she told me, was that it's a terrible thing that we live in a culture where this sexual event that occurred in her twenties could cause her to feel shame that has persisted for the rest of my life. She said that this was the sort of thing she loved Arthur for.

Aunt Birdie had developed a pattern of waking several times during the night and reading until she fell asleep again with the book still in her hands. Arthur now slept in the guest bedroom so Birdie could feel free to turn on the light to read in the middle of the night. They had never before slept in separate bedrooms. When Arthur came to their bedroom in the morning to help her with something or just to talk, he seemed awkward. "He keeps his distance from me, placing his chair close to the foot of the bed."

I was surprised when Aunt Birdie then said that she was considering moving to a retirement home. Birdie's friends, Julia and Cecily, had looked into such homes in the suburbs because Birdie couldn't afford one in the city. They found one in Pelham that they agreed was a pleasant enough place where the staff seemed respectful of the residents. Birdie said, "The apartment is no longer my home. It's now Arthur's and Nell's home. I don't want to live there any longer."

I didn't hear from Aunt Birdie until a few days after the move occurred, which came much more quickly than I'd expected. When she called, she said, "Pelham is a nondescript town that hasn't decided whether to be residential or industrial. I suppose I'll rarely visit the town itself. The room is ample. The furniture is early monastic and there are no locks on the doors. They ignore Do Not Disturb signs. The other residents seem quiet, but friendly enough. Quite a number are severely demented. Julia and Cecily came to visit. Arthur says he'll be over."

In response to my question about how she's getting around, she said, "Slowly. The pain is there in my hip, but it's no longer the principal thing in my life that isn't the way it once was. I'm fine with a cane when I'm not tired. When I'm tired, I use a walker. There's a tightly woven carpet on the floor that prevents me from catching the tips of the walker."

Birdie was speaking quickly as she did when she was upset. She didn't mention Arthur. I assumed she was trying to get acclimated to no longer living with him.

In time, Birdie settled into her new residence. Her intelligence and kindness made her appealing to both the staff and some of the forty-odd residents in the home. She said that the staff by and large respected her privacy though they were not to be deterred when distributing medications. Other residents sought her company. Agnes, who lived in the room next to her, cried through the night in the most heartbreaking way, begging to be allowed to go home to live with her husband who died fifteen years ago. Birdie comforted her most nights.

As we talked during the subsequent months, Birdie began to make friends at the home, but she was put off by the way the residents behaved like children completely dependent on the staff.

Birdie said she'd been less than honest with me when she told me that she hadn't had children because of her TB, and later, because of her work and Arthur's. The truth was that she never had wanted children from the time she was a small child. "I didn't play with dolls as a girl. I liked Nancy Drew but didn't find her very interesting. I wasn't frightened by the fact that her mother had died. I envied her that. My mother was depressed, and hospitalized repeatedly. She was not at all prepared to be a mother and was badly in need of one. I, as the eldest girl, took on the task of being a mother to my younger sister. I loved her very much, but being a mother was a job I would never again let myself be saddled with."

Birdie took her meals in the dining room with the other residents. She told me about the friends she'd made and about the people who bored her. "I sometimes feel that the worst sin a human being can commit is the sin of being boring." Beatrice was a resident whose name came up frequently in Birdie's conversations with me. She said Beatrice was at once a delicate soul and irrepressible. She was different from the people with whom she and Arthur socialized. They were almost exclusively doctors and professors. And she was different from Julia and Cecily, professors' wives, who Birdie said were trying to reinvent themselves after their children had left home. Beatrice was lovely. "A pleasure to talk with, a pleasure to spend time with." She said that Beatrice's memory was poor, but she was certainly not demented. She would forget not only conversations she'd had with Birdie, she'd forget having seen her earlier the same day or the preceding day.

This pained Birdie. "Beatrice is someone you'd love to meet but you feel you don't bring your fair share to the conversation with her. She is well read but you'd never know it unless you mentioned a book or a play. Even then, she is more interested in hearing what you think than in telling you what she thinks. She was a high school English teacher until her failing memory forced her to retire. I'm giving you her CV because I'm at a loss to know how to tell you who she is."

One day, Birdie said, "I love Beatrice. I'm wary of telling you that because I don't think you will understand what the word love means in that sentence. It's not to be dismissed as old lady love. It has a depth that draws on the sum of all the passions and heartbreaks of a lifetime. I don't think you can understand what it feels like. You have other kinds of love to live, precious ones that I sorely miss. But at my age, this is a great gift. I feel very fortunate. And there's nothing to lose, which gives me freedom ... Are you still there?"

I told her I was.

"Good, I thought I was committing that worst of all sins."

"I'm listening, feeling glad for you, and a bit envious, I have to say. I'm trying to imagine what you're describing, and can't quite. My experience with love is limited. I feel I've led an economy-class life because that's all that I'm able to afford."

"Oh Leonard, dear, dear Leonard. You are such a sweet man, a decent man, an intelligent man, an interesting man, a good-hearted man, a handsome man, though you may not know it. For me, those are the most important things. But I'm getting tired now. Please excuse me." Click.

I received a call from Adele Elise, the chief nurse of the home where Birdie lived. Birdie apparently listed me as the first person to call in case of an emergency. This struck me as odd but understandable given the difficulty she and Arthur were having. Maybe she didn't want to bother her two friends. Adele told me Birdie had had an accident and had been taken to a local hospital where her arm had been x-rayed. They found that she had not fractured it but had badly sprained her wrist. She'd been given morphine for the pain and would not be able to talk with me until tomorrow.

Adele sounded knowledgeable and experienced, as well as a bit defensive. I thanked her for calling.

When I spoke to Birdie the next day, she was not the least bit groggy, as I'd expected her to be. There was excitement in her voice of a sort I had never heard before. "Beatrice and I had a bit of an adventure yesterday, the two of us were out walking with our canes. We took a path through a small area of woods and then over a small wooden bridge that crossed the creek. We'd been talking about doing this. I can see the woods from my room and can hear the creek at night. All was going well until the tip of Beatrice's cane slipped on some wet leaves and she began to fall. I took her arm to soften the fall, but I went over with her. She wasn't hurt, but my arm was causing me a good deal of pain, so I couldn't get to my feet. The two of us were there on the ground stuck in the wet leaves on the path, helpless as turtles on their backs. A woman who saw us was very good to us. She said that she thought we were best off where we were until she could get help from someone stronger than she was. Before very long the police arrived. The two policemen were gentlemanly. They helped us up and took us to the ER. I called the home. What a fuss they made. When the police returned us to the home, the staff told us we would be "restricted," their word for "punished." Would you believe that? Punished at our age. They said that we would no longer be allowed to walk the paved path into the woods. I don't care."

Birdie told me the following day that Beatrice did care. She cared so deeply that she promptly and definitively forgot the adventure altogether. This was disturbing to Birdie for whom the outing had been nothing short of an elopement. She denied that saying, "Of course, I don't confound what we did to an elopement to wed, but it was, for me, symbolic, a declaration of independence if you like."

Birdie became despondent in the face of Beatrice's withdrawal after the outing. She pined for Beatrice who sometimes smiled at her, but her smile now, Birdie told me, seemed to be without warmth. Birdie rarely asked me for my opinion, but she now asked if I thought that Beatrice was angry at her for causing her such a fright and for causing her to be scolded by the staff. Had the incident sent a shockwave of some sort through Beatrice? I told her that I couldn't imagine that a fall and a scolding would cause Beatrice to love her any less. She thanked me for my thoughts, but it was clear that she dismissed what I said as the thoughts of someone who couldn't understand the situation she was in.

Birdie stopped calling me and did not pick up the phone in her room when I called. I spoke to Adele at the home several times. She said that Birdie sat silently at mealtime and often did not show up for meals at all.

I made preparations to fly out to see her. They told Birdie I was coming, but she seemed uninterested. When the taxi dropped me off at the retirement home, I saw that the central building was a large Victorian house to which had been added two modern single-story extensions, as if wings had been stuck on a bird.

I was escorted to Birdie's room where the nurse accompanying me knocked on the door. No response. She knocked again and we could hear some movement in the room. When Birdie opened the door, I was met by a small old woman with thin white hair that poorly hid her bright pinkish scalp. She looked more ancient than I'd remembered her. Her back was bent forward from its base to the neck and her face was a network of minute lines etched in soft flesh.

"Birdie, it's good to see you."

"I'm too old for lies."

"I came because I'm worried about how you've been after the accident ... ."

"Words are important, Leonard. It wasn't an accident, it was an adventure."

"An adventure that went wrong."

"No, it didn't go wrong, it did anything but go wrong. How can two people crossing a stream be thought of as wrong? We're old. We fell. Old people fall. That doesn't make it wrong."

"Birdie, it wasn't the fall or the punishment that is disappointing you, it's Beatrice shutting you out afterward that's troubling you. That's what's painful."

"You're too young to know anything about love ... That's not fair. You've been wonderful to me, and that counts as love. I'm sorry I said that. Love is a strange word. It means something different in every sentence in which it's used, and rightly so. Not using the word love doesn't mean that it isn't felt. In a state of passion, it may be left unsaid because it's inadequate. My love for Arthur once was passionate and he and I almost never said the word to one another.

I'm not going to tell you what that word means with Beatrice. I couldn't if I tried.

"You don't know what it's like to be a woman. I was pretty when I was young, and there was nothing better than that, except that I wasn't really seen. I couldn't really see myself, but that was all right at the time. As I got a bit older, I could see my beauty slipping away from me. I slept with those medical residents to prove to myself that men found me pretty, though they would have slept with me if I hadn't been pretty."

"You're upset that Beatrice has wiped you from her mind, but there's no reason to think that's so."

"Why don't we have some dinner."

The dining tables were set up in the room used for physical exercise in the morning, for music and the arts in the afternoon, and for guest speakers or musicians in the evening. There were six round tables adorned with white tablecloths and cloth napkins, each surrounded by eight chairs. The staff wore casual work clothes. Some residents needed help feeding themselves.

A few of the residents were studying me. I was perhaps the most interesting thing that had happened that day or perhaps in weeks. Many stole glances. Some seemed to expect me not to be able to stay in this room for very long with strange people like themselves. Still others seemed to look at me with longing because, I imagined, no one came to visit them.

On seeing me looking around the room, Birdie said, "Please excuse all of us for being old. We can't help it."

"Birdie, I don't deserve that."

"I'm sorry, I really don't know what you're thinking ... you'd lie rather than tell me the truth about what you're thinking."

"I don't make a habit of lying," I said.

"I apologize. That was unfair and uncalled for. I'd be the age of your father's mother, my sister, your grandmother if she were still alive."

"Yes, I suppose."

"Don't suppose, I am," Birdie insisted. "Your grandmother on your mother's side, Rosaline, was in a retirement home during the last year of her life because she couldn't afford home care in her apartment. Isn't that right?"

"Yes."

"You and your brother could have afforded to pay for home care, and you didn't. Am I right?"

"No, you're not right," he said. "Bernard and I didn't think that it was safe for her to be at home. She had fallen quite a number of times and had been very lucky she hadn't broken anything. She needed 24-hour homecare, and we couldn't afford that."

Birdie knew that she had located a pocket of pain in me and had poked a needle into it. She must have sensed that I had doubts about whether I could have afforded home care for my grandmother. At the time, I didn't think I could afford it, but I've come to think differently, particularly because she died six months after she left the house she'd lived in most of her life.

"That's not … It was mean-spirited of me to say that," she said quietly. "You're right, I don't know the whole story and have no right to judge you. I lose friends for saying whatever comes to my mind. Other people have filters between their thoughts and their mouths. I've lost whatever filter I once had."

We finished dinner and I went to stay at a local hotel.

I didn't sleep much that night. Had I been protective of my grandmother or was I neglectful — not simply neglectful, outright stingy, self-centered? I could have afforded homecare, not easily, but I could have done it, for a while. She never once asked me to help her financially. She trusted me and accepted the decisions I made.

The next morning, I had an impulse to return to California, but quickly came to my senses. I met Birdie in the room where we'd dined the previous evening. Residents were scattered around the room, some at tables playing board games, some sitting in chairs deep in their own thoughts, others seemingly incapable of thought, some in pairs, and still others with staff members assembling jigsaw puzzles. The whole scene was otherworldly, silent in a way that suggested the stillness of absolute zero, of existence lived without words, not because there aren't words to express ideas and feelings, but because there aren't ideas and feelings to express.

Birdie sat alone on a chair pulled to the side of one of the large round tables.

"I should say hello, but I don't feel like it," Birdie said as if talking to herself.

"What do you feel like?"

"I feel like hell. I don't know if I feel like screaming obscenities or disappearing."

"I'd like to meet Beatrice."

Birdie fumbled before saying, "I don't know where she is."

"Of course, you do. I asked a member of the staff to point her out to me. She's right over there."

"You have no right."

"I do."

"What Beatrice is to me is my business and I'd appreciate your staying out of it."

"I'm going to go over and introduce myself to her."

"Don't you dare."

"Would you introduce me to her?"

"Let me think."

"What are you afraid of? That she won't recognize you, which is ridiculous."

"No, I'm afraid she will."

"And that you'll see she wants nothing to do with you?"

"Don't talk to me as if I'm a child."

Birdie got to her feet unsteadily and took my arm. We slowly, deliberately crossed the room. Beatrice was alone and had her back to us. I broke the silence, saying her name. Beatrice slowly turned and gave a benign smile to Birdie, but completely ignored me.

Birdie said, "I'm sorry to interrupt your morning, but my nephew, Leonard, said he wanted to meet you."

"How nice it is to meet you, Leonard," she said with so little feeling that it could have been the recorded voice of an answering machine.

"Birdie tells me that the two of you had quite an adventure."

"Leonard, what gives you the right," Birdie said.

"Yes, we had quite a time of it. And I had a fall. Birdie may have told you. They scolded us. But they can't take from us what's beyond their reach. Isn't that right, Birdie?"

"Beatrice, where have you been?"

"Right here, haven't I?"

"You have, but you've seemed like you wanted nothing to do with me."

"What's given you that impression? Of course, I want to see you."

The following day I returned to New York. The flight seemed endless because I felt as if I was returning home with less than I had left with. I felt utterly depleted.

—

I called Birdie a few days later. She didn't answer her phone. On calling the reception line of the home, I was told that Birdie had again become sullen and withdrawn, hardly herself. I didn't ask about Beatrice because I had no right to inquire into her life.

I continued to try to reach her by phone for a few days but was shunted to the recorded voice of an answering machine, a female voice, not Birdie's. More than a week went by before Birdie finally accepted my phone call.

She answered by simply saying, "Yes."

"Birdie, I've been trying to reach you all week …."

"I'm not a child, you know."

"Yes, I know that, but I also worry about you."

"Don't"

"Why have you not been answering your phone?"

"I haven't wanted to speak with anyone," she said.

"Would you tell me why?"

"I haven't known what I would say."

"Just saying hello is fine with me," I said.

"That's kind of you, but I don't know what to add to what I've already said."

"Would it be all right if I come to see you again?" I asked.

"We're doing all right talking by phone. I do appreciate your talking with me."

Not knowing what to say, I heard myself saying, "I've missed talking with you this past week. I'd been looking forward to hearing more of what happened during and after the walk you took with Beatrice."

"I told you I don't want to talk about anything, including that, especially that. I know I'm not being pleasant, Leonard, but I don't have any wish to talk about myself. Why don't you tell me about yourself."

I was startled by her question because our conversations from the outset had been almost exclusively about her.

"You know I've divorced and see my children, Leah and Jimmy, every other weekend."

"I'm sorry."

"This has been in the offing for years, so it's a matter of making it work for each of the four of us."

"How does it work?"

I sighed as I decided how much to say. It was impossible for me to answer the question because I didn't know how it was working for any of us. Whether it was working for me would have been like asking a patient anesthetized, on an operating table, belly open, guts hanging out, how it was going for him. I could have replied by saying something meaningless like "Well enough" or "It's been hard," but I tried to be as honest as I could.

"It's been an agony. I don't sleep well as I go over and over what I could have done to change what's happening and I try to imagine what I might have done and what I can do now. I try to imagine how I might change to make things better for my children, and then decide that I'm stuck with myself, but that doesn't mean I can't do better at that, and so it goes round and round. You get a sense of what life's been like for me: a great deal of second-guessing, self-hatred, and self-pity."

"Don't do that to yourself."

"Do what?"

"Punish yourself. It's worse than nothing. Doing nothing leaves things as they are, punishing yourself feels like you're doing something, but it's making things worse."

And so that conversation ended. I hadn't liked talking about my troubles. I'm not good at talking about myself.

Weeks later, Birdie returned to her pattern of not picking up my phone calls at all. Adele told me that Birdie had returned to being her usual personable self, so she didn't understand why Birdie was shutting me out.

———

One Sunday evening, I received a call.

It was Adele. "Birdie isn't in her room or anywhere else."

"When was the last time you saw her?"

"At dinner. She sat alone as she does sometimes."

"Is there anything missing from her room?"

"She took her winter coat and handbag. Those are the only things that seem to be missing."

"Have you alerted the police?"

"No, we wanted to talk with you first. To see if you knew where she might have gone. It's not just Birdie who's missing, she and Beatrice seem to have left together."

"Call the police now and please keep me informed about what's happening, even if it's the middle of the night."

During the days that followed, I felt as if I were living in a cold, damp cave lit by grayish light. There was no news of their whereabouts. To me, it felt as if it were a matter of two old people feeling free to go off on their own, without telling anyone, because they were already dead to everyone. Birdie had little to look forward to at the home.

The staff of the retirement home was in a state of panic. Two residents were unaccounted for, which was far worse than their having died: dying is natural and inevitable, but being unaccounted for is not. There was genuine concern among those who knew Birdie and Beatrice, but it was different from worry about children who'd gone missing. Birdie and Beatrice were faltering flames, not the delicate new glow of children. They would do what they were doing until they were located, at which point they may be declared incompetent and have their few remaining rights taken from them. Such a thing would be a death sentence for Birdie.

I was told by staff members that there was excitement among the residents of the home. Had they gone to South America or a Caribbean Island? Maybe Tahiti. The plane ride itself was talked about with enthusiasm: you can buy the little bottles of Johnny Walker Red or Gilbey's Gin to which you can add tonic and a squeeze of fresh lime or add tomato juice and a sprig of celery. You can get two drinks if you want. More would get you drunk and it's not pleasant to be drunk on a long plane ride. There was speculation about what they took with them: they wouldn't need suitcases. A carry-on would be enough because you can buy what you need when you get there. Beatrice has money, someone said. Not a problem. All they need is some cash for the first few days and then transfer money from the New York bank to a local one.

I took the plane to Kennedy a few days later, rented a car, and slept at the Motel 6 on the interstate not far from the home: a bed, a round table, two chairs, an old TV, and a bathroom, all in a style that seemed to be saying to the guest that the rooms are furnished in the cheapest way possible in order to keep the price of the room as low as possible, which is what you want, isn't it?

I drove to the home the next morning to talk with some of the residents. Perhaps Birdie or Beatrice had confided in one or two of them, telling them what they were planning, though I doubted it. My mood had become one of acceptance, even admiration, of what Birdie and Beatrice were doing, whatever that might be. It turned out that the residents I spoke with were either too demented or too identified with the courage of the two "escapees" to tell me anything to help me determine where they might have gone.

Beatrice's family, which consisted of two sons, one of whom lived in Toronto and the other in Austen, were notified of her absence. They were concerned but didn't know how they could help.

Adele told me that the police had asked if Beatrice and Birdie were competent to make decisions for themselves. They had told the police that Birdie was competent, but Beatrice was not. The police asked if Beatrice was competent to make the decision to leave with Birdie. If she weren't, this would be considered a kidnapping. Adele, not wanting to designate Birdie as a kidnapper, said that Beatrice could make that decision, so a hunt by the police was deemed unnecessary.

I returned to the West Coast. On arriving at my apartment, I found a message on my answering machine from Birdie saying that she and Beatrice were well and perfectly capable of caring for themselves so she would appreciate it if the staff at the retirement home and I would accept the fact that she and Beatrice were safe and had a right to live on their own if they chose. The background noise sounded as if Birdie was calling from a pay phone in a public space. I relayed Birdie's message to Adele who was beside herself with anger. "It doesn't look good when two residents run off like this. Heads are gonna roll. They must know that and not give a damn."

———

Weeks and then months went by without another word from Birdie or Beatrice. I wasn't worried that they were in severe distress. They knew how to get help if they needed it. I did wonder where they were and how they were getting on.

I received a phone call from Birdie five-and-a-half months after she and Beatrice disappeared. She spoke to me as if we had talked only a few days earlier. She said that Beatrice had died in her sleep the previous night. Birdie said that she still held her New York State medical license and had renewed the drugs Beatrice had been taking. When I asked where she was, she grudgingly said she was in a town on Lake Placid. I asked her if there was anything she'd like me to do. She told me that she was very tired and would appreciate my dealing with the mortuary. Beatrice was in the arm-chair in which she was seated when she died. Birdie gave me the address and phone number of the house where she was living and the name of the mortuary she wanted me to contact.

"What would you like me to ask them to do?"

"Just tell them to prepare the body for cremation. That's what Beatrice wanted. I'll sign whatever papers need signing."

"Would you tell me what you've been doing?"

"Living a quiet, peaceful life. It's been quite wondrous."

I told Adele what I'd heard from Birdie so they could tell Beat-rice's sons that she had been located and that she had died the pre-vious night. I was told by Adele that Beatrice had been disappoint-ed by the fact that her children and grandchildren had not come to visit in recent years, though they did talk by phone.

Birdie told me that Beatrice said she didn't mind if a memorial service was held at the retirement home, but Birdie had no interest in organizing one herself.

The staff and residents of the home held a memorial service which Birdie attended. This was the only time Birdie returned to the home. Birdie was cordial to the staff and warm with other resi-dents who missed Beatrice and wanted to know where she and Birdie had been living.

I was told by Adele that several of the residents spoke at the service. One said she was proud of Birdie and Beatrice for "running away" from the home. A staff member who had worked closely with Beatrice said that she had never met a kinder person than Beatrice. She described Beatrice reading for hours to a resident who was blind. The man's life had been devoted to editing at a publishing house which had afforded him a very satisfying life, though he hadn't married. But the loss of his eyesight had left him in deep despair. Others had offered to read to him, but he had turned them away. Beatrice had opened a book she thought he'd like and began to read. At first, he pretended not to be interested, but he couldn't continue that ruse for very long. He sat there in a state of deep satisfaction as she read to him each day until the day he died. He left all his books to Beatrice who gave them to the home.

I knew Birdie was doing what she could to live in a world without Beatrice. She was temporarily staying in The Roosevelt Hotel in New York. Birdie's friends, Julia and Cecily, were trying to help Birdie find a new place to live.

After another month or so, Birdie called me. Her voice was subdued and patient. "You didn't know Beatrice. She is a person impossible to describe. She set the tone of every room she walked into. She was kind, but she was more than kind. She was gracious in her kindness."

I told Birdie that it wasn't necessary for her to fill me in on what had happened. That was hers and Beatrice's. She said she wanted to tell me.

"When we left the home that day in March, we had no second thoughts about what we were doing. We were old but we were perfectly capable of living on our own. We'd been residents at the home because it was convenient for us and for everyone else. The place had its value, but the convenience it provided began to feel oppressive to us, particularly after they scolded us for walking across the bridge and prohibited us from doing it again. Of course, it wasn't the fact that we couldn't cross the bridge again, it was that they were prohibiting us from doing so — at our age. We had a little time remaining in our lives which we insisted on making our own. This wasn't a Bonnie and Clyde campaign, it was something else. I don't have a name for it."

"Where did you go that first night?"

"We took a room in a little hotel in the Bowery. Not a flop house, a nice clean place. What an exciting night that was. Our first time together out of the reach of the 'authorities' at the home. I have to admit we felt like little children who had run away from home. But we genuinely did not want to be found and be brought back as naughty children. We took a cab to the Village. We could get around, if slowly, with our canes. The indignities of old age.

"The Village is quite posh now, not like the '60s when people were living on couches in run-down places on Christopher Street and the Avenues. The places each of us had gone when we were young were still there: The Purple Onion, the Village Gate, and I forget the names of the other places. We weren't frightened on the street because we had nothing to lose. That state of mind is one of the gifts of old age. We were in a state of mind in which there's no past and no future. Young people, like you, are living in a future they will never actually live. Their dreams of the future are tranquilizers for the terror they are feeling now. I remember being mesmerized by the birds that came to the ornate concrete bird bath we had in our garden when I was growing up. I'd watch a bird land on the lip of the bath. Before he'd drink, he stood as still as he could and turned his head more than fifty times, this way and that, completely around before he'd lean his head forward and drink for a moment and then return to surveying. As an old lady, I don't have to survey. You may not understand that because you're still young."

"The future I live in isn't much better than the present."

"I'm sorry. I had no right to tell you how you live. I was confused and desperate when I was young. You're not me. You are a very bright and compassionate man."

"So, tell me what you and Beatrice did."

"Beatrice had been to Upstate New York as a child with her parents but had not been there for seventy years. We knew that if we didn't like it there, we were free to go somewhere else. Beatrice was well-off financially because her husband had been a successful lawyer, so we didn't have to worry about money. We lived on much less money than what they charge at the retirement home. I hate the name 'retirement home.' It's not a place you go when you retire from a job, it's a place you go when you retire from life.

"I had trepidations about Lake Placid because I don't like the cold and I knew they had very cold winters. But Beatrice was set on it, so we went. We hired a driver, a very nice man, Manuel, who not only drove us up there, but he helped us find a reliable real estate agent who showed us houses that were for rent.

"There were plenty of places to rent. New Yorkers go up there for the summer and leave the houses empty the rest of the year. So, the houses are fully furnished down to sheets and towels and dishcloths. It felt like we were excited newlyweds when we went to the supermarket for the first time together. You have to understand we had never once bought anything together.

"The rented homes furnish everything you need to the point that they kill your desire to buy anything. You don't need anything. That's not a natural state of affairs. Animals ... even plants ... always need something. Killing not only one's desire but one's need, is to kill you off ... I'm getting distracted and losing track of what I'm saying. Please be honest with me if you've heard enough."

"I want to hear more," I said. "I'm listening with a good deal of admiration because I've never experienced the sense of freedom and exhilaration that you're describing, and I don't know that I ever will."

"Of course, you will," she said. "If I were your age, I'd love to go out with you ... I don't mean to embarrass you. I'm too old now to be embarrassed because I no longer feel shame. That, too, is a gift of old age. To live without shame is a wondrous thing, particularly for a woman who was taught to be ashamed of so many things, not just her body, but everything feminine about her. I sound like a feminist, but I'm not.

"There's a difference between the sexes. Life would be so very uninteresting without it. Women love to make themselves into Christmas trees to be decorated with clothes and jewelry. A ridiculous thing, but a wondrous art. And I enjoy these shared pleasures with other women. Men love to fight wars on the battlefields, in baseball stadiums and football fields, anywhere they can get into fights, which are as meaningless as the Christmas tree game women enjoy. Now I'm going off again."

"You liked Lake Placid?"

"No, I didn't like the lake or the town very much, it couldn't be less interesting. I liked living with Beatrice in our house. Something you may not understand is that being close to another person when you're old doesn't involve talking nearly as much as it does when you're younger. In old age, the most profound form of closeness comes in sitting together in silence, just feeling light from the sun come through the window crossing the final three yards of the journey that it's taken seemingly for the sole purpose of illuminating the room and warming the faces and shoulders and legs of the two of you sitting there."

It was now close to midnight on the East Coast so we ended our call. The story Birdie was telling was a eulogy not only for Beatrice, and not only for the couple Birdie and Beatrice had made, but also for Birdie herself.

I had grown genuinely fond of Birdie but I didn't know if she could hear that in my voice. My voice sounded unfamiliar to me, softer, less constrained, using a fuller register of sound.

Ordinarily, I would wait until the weekend to speak again with Birdie, but the patterns that fit previous days didn't apply now. I called in the early evening of East Coast time. I asked how she was. She said she was being carried as if by a sail filled taut with the wind. I told her I wanted to hear more about her time with Beatrice.

"There was nothing we had to do, so everything we did was done because we wanted to do it. There were chores, but even the chores, especially the chores, were exciting because they were the bones of the life we were making together. We had no patience for people who, unsolicited, tried to help us or sell us something. We told them to respect our privacy. And they honored our request. Tradesmen and realtors and the like. I know it wasn't easy for you to be in the dark about what had become of us. You're not a controlling person, but you are protective, you know.

"We walked the paved path at the edge of the lake when the weather permitted. The lake is beautiful in its winter clothes: solid gray-blue ice across the entire expanse, skeletons of trees on the shore, grasses poking through the ice. The birches and aspen with their peeling bark stand between the huge evergreens. I know that all of this sounds romantic and sentimental, but I'm just telling you what it looked like to me."

I said she sounded in love.

"Time hardly existed. I didn't know what day of the week or which month of the year it was. I told time only by the brightness of the clouds and the occasional appearance of the sun. We went to bed when we were tired and got up when we felt like it. Our bodies were also a form of time. They were like very old machinery that was breaking down. Beatrice never talked about her health, so I had to make inferences from her appearance, her appetite, her stamina, and her winces in response to jolts of pain. Our walks became shorter, and she ate less and less. We had an unstated agreement that we would not be consulting doctors and taking new medicines. Our bodies would carry us as far as they could go. We weren't afraid of dying. Beatrice's memory never was an issue because she rarely had need for it. Everything that happened was happening now and we had no need of the past or the future. The two of us were all there ever was and all there ever would be.

"When summer approached, we had to move to a house owned by someone who wasn't going to use it that summer. It was a smaller house set back a few blocks from the lake. You can't imagine how little the house mattered to us. The house was just a place where we were living together. You might also wonder if the intensity of the feeling of newness and excitement of our life together had worn off by this time. It had changed a little, it had become less frothy. The trips to the supermarket were still a novelty, still with the feeling of newlyweds playing house. It's when you stop playing house at the supermarket that life gets dull and eventually oppressive.

"It's embarrassing the way I'm going on here about two old ladies living together at Lake Placid. That's the stuff of comedy. I suppose the months we spent there could be seen as comedy. We didn't take ourselves seriously. It's not as if we were modeling ourselves for anyone. There wasn't really anyone who mattered other than the two of us. That was new for me. I'd always lived with a sense that someone was watching me, judging me, a person who knew who I should be and the ways I was falling short of it. For those months, only the two of us existed. We could forget about the rest of the people in the world — the supermarket cashier, the real estate agent, the phone company — because they were doing their job. The same was true of the appliances in the house. They weren't something to be thought about unless something broke, which rarely happened. But when it did happen, we were taken by surprise, as if woken from a sleep.

"Leonard, I apologize for asking you this once again, but I can't imagine how a man much younger than I am would be interested in the lives of old ladies."

"I think that your calling yourself an old lady feels almost like a profanity," I said. "It's such a contemptuous phrase bringing with it an image of femininity in old age as a failure of femininity, an unseemly state devoid of anything interesting and compelling and beautiful. It hurts me to hear you do that to yourself."

Birdie was silent for a while before saying, "You're very bright and very sweet, you know ... It's getting late for me. Let's talk more another time." Click.

I meant what I said to Birdie about her use of the term old lady. She seemed feminine to me in a lovely way, not devoid of sexuality.

———

Arthur didn't ask her to come home to live with him when she returned from Lake Placid. He knew better. After some looking, Birdie took a sprawling two-bedroom apartment on 79th and Central Park West. The building had a dining room on the ground floor where she could have her meals when she chose to. Beatrice had left a good deal of her estate to Birdie, so finances were not a concern.

A month or so later, when I called, Birdie said that she was living among an array of boxes and pieces of furniture that looked like farm animals wandering over a field. She said that Nell, the housekeeper, was going to help her unpack. "Nell is welcome to hide anything she chooses because everything is already hidden from me."

Birdie said that she wanted to tell me more about the life she and Beatrice had had together because there was no one else she cared to tell, and she wanted to tell the story so it would not die with her. She said she didn't know why that mattered so much to her, but it did.

The part of the story she wanted me to hear was the last part of the life she and Beatrice had together. "We never talked about the past, Beatrice and I. There was no forgetting because there was no remembering. I probably have told you that before. I don't know if I can tell you what it was like when Beatrice's transient ischemic attacks began to occur. We were fully aware this was happening but neither of us was thrown by it. We both knew that Beatrice did not want to bring doctors into her life. She accepted death — actually, it's not death but dying — as intrinsic to life. She didn't want the last part of her life to be a period filled with doctors' visits and new medications and their side effects. Instead, there were experiences of dizziness and falling followed by periods of confusion. That was that. These attacks were what they were, like anything else.

"One afternoon, Beatrice and I were sitting in the living room of the second house we rented. I was reading. Beatrice didn't like reading after her eyesight began to fail her and she couldn't bear to hear other people read books to her because she wanted to create the sounds of the voices in her own head, and not have them created by someone else. We were sitting there as we did most days.

Beatrice often closed her eyes as we sat. I noticed the absence of the sound of her breathing and even before I went over to check on her, I knew she had died. This will sound strange, but the very first feeling I had was not the sadness of her dying but the rightness of her dying silently while doing what she took pleasure in doing. I sat down in the chair next to hers and remained there for a long time, I don't know how long, but the light in the room changed from the dull light of the afternoon to the murkiness of dusk. I didn't want to live any longer. There was nothing in life for me except the business of surviving: obtaining food, shelter, and clothing. Those necessities felt like too much trouble to bother with. If I could have died by saying the word, I would have. Don't mistake what I'm saying for the end of a tragedy. It's the end of a rich existence the last part of which was just as I would have hoped for. I called the police, a procedure I'd learned as a doctor when I made occasional house calls for families of friends when a member of their family died. The police were polite. They said that I should take as much time with Beatrice as I liked. They gave me the name of a mortuary that would pick up the body. When they left, I called you."

"I'm honored you chose me to call."

"Such a formal word."

"Yes, I meant it that way. It means a lot to me that I came to mind at that moment, at such an important moment."

We were both silent for quite a long time. I said, "What now?"

"That's all there is. Now. Talking with you now. I don't know what I'll do after now."

Birdie and I continued to talk by phone, but in the months that followed her voice became weaker and weaker. I flew to New York to see her because, despite her protestations, I did worry about her. She wasn't taking care of herself. There were still unopened boxes piled in corners and furniture strewn around.

I was not surprised to receive the call a week later telling me she had died. The woman who came weekly to help Birdie with paying bills and arranging for service people to repair broken appliances found her. This woman told me that she hoped that Birdie had died not very long before she came for her weekly visit. I told her I thought Birdie had not minded waiting.

A memorial service for Birdie was held at the retirement home, which I attended. There was a feeling of sadness mixed with a bit of resentment that Birdie had betrayed them by choosing not to live with them when she returned from Lake Placid. I was surprised when Adele asked me if I would like to say something. As I made my way to the front of the room, I tried to organize what I might say but was unable to, so I spoke spontaneously.

"What I'm feeling now is sadness because the world is an emptier place for me because Birdie isn't in it. I don't have a way of describing what Birdie taught me, how knowing her has changed me, other than to say it has to do with seeing and feeling things in a way that is freer, richer, more colorful."

What I didn't say was that there was one thing that she did at the end of her life that hurt me deeply. She could have told me where she and Beatrice were living. I would have kept her secret.

— THE WAY IT IS —

She'd actually once felt proud of him. He had refused to take a job at her family's company. He could be charming. People liked him. Before they met, he had worked as a salesman selling time to radio stations. She couldn't keep straight in her mind who was paying whom for what in those sales. He was a disappointment; so was she. She could kill him with her words and glances, or so she thought. He was a commuter, never missing the 7:37 train that stopped at seven stations before reaching Grand Central. Gray fedora, camel coat, blue pin-striped suit. He'd grown up on 76th and West End Avenue, not far from where her family lived before they moved to Park Avenue. He was from a good Jewish family; she was from a better one. She went to the Columbia Girls' School; he, seven years older than she, had gone to the Columbia Boys' School. She hated every minute of it. Fat, pimply, invisible to the smart girls, a target of the pretty girls. He'd almost flunked out.

The draft notice arrived at their apartment on West 21st Street three months after their honeymoon. It happened quickly, decisively. Draft notice, order to report to Fort Dix, troop train to Mayport Base, troop ship to the Pacific, stationed off the east coast of India waiting for four years for orders to invade Japan. He and the other soldiers never said the words "virtually certain death." Didn't have to. He wrote long letters, which she saved, along with pencil drawings a friend of his had made of his lower bunk: clothesline draped from one bedpost to the other, socks drying, Indian houseboy under his bed grinning knowingly. She liked him, even loved him, she thought.

After the war, he sold life insurance, at first to veterans, who, like him, had children soon after returning from the war. For these veterans, their own mortality was not obscured by romantic fairytales, it was a beast they knew intimately. Using the money her father had left her, he paid the premiums of the life insurance he sold to these veterans with the understanding that they would repay him when they could.

She trusted him. Didn't worry about what he was doing. Never questioned him. He said he felt proud, not of himself, but of the men to whom he'd sold the insurance policies: not a single man failed to pay back the money he had lent them.

She, as a girl, was plump and her mother never let her forget it. She, Livia, and he, Wes, met at a party thrown by a mutual friend soon after she graduated from college. She rarely went to parties — not invited to most of them. When Wes asked her to marry him, she'd only known him for two weeks. He was handsome, in a Humphrey Bogart sort of way, and that was all she could be certain of. He was hurt by the fact that she didn't immediately say "yes." He gave her 48 hours to make up her mind. She accepted because she doubted any other man would ever ask her to marry him. Which of them received the worse end of that deal, she often wondered. He looked very handsome at the wedding, which was one thing her mother couldn't deny, much as she disapproved of this man who, though Jewish, hadn't gone to college.

They bought their house in the New York suburbs a year after Wes returned from the Pacific. Livia lived in that house for the next seventy-two years. Standing up to the seller of the house was Wes's finest hour, she thought. When they were being shown around the house by the real estate agent, the owner sat stolidly in the living room: "Jews come and go through this house, but they never want to buy it." Wes replied, "This Jew's going to buy it."

The house had an inviting living room: beautiful in a simple sort of way. There was no dining room. On the ground floor, there was the master bedroom, which was dark, with small casement windows and a low ceiling traversed by dark wood beams. The bathroom was hardly large enough for two people to use at the same time. Two small bedrooms on the second floor. There was a much smaller house across the patio, the "Little House," as they called it, which had been the studio of the artist who designed and built the pair of houses thirty years earlier.

———

Wes was one of the men Mike greeted on Saturday mornings when men dropped in to buy gas, or to check on the progress of their car in the body shop, or just to chat. Livia had once or twice been in the car with Wes when he pulled into the service station. She resisted when Wes invited her to get out of the car to say hello to Mike. She'd met him a few times when dropping off one of their cars for repair. Mike always asked someone, usually the youngest kid working for him, to drive her home. During the few times their paths crossed, Mike had been cordial, having no trouble making social conversation, while she struggled to find something to say. She comforted herself by dismissing him as a lower middle-class second-generation Italian who owed it to his parents to accrue enough money to buy a house in a good neighborhood and produce a large crop of grandchildren. She imagined his family had Mafia connections. Livia also suspected that his gas station and body shop had underworld connections — maybe money laundering, though she didn't know exactly how that worked. He's the most successful kind of con artist, she thought, a con artist who doesn't know he's a con artist.

For Wes, Mike was good at what he did and deserved credit for it. His greeting felt genuinely warm when Wes dropped by on Saturdays. He liked the way Mike shook hands firmly with his right hand while gripping Wes's left forearm with his left hand and looking him straight in the eye.

It was a surprise to Livia, one Saturday afternoon, when she saw an old Ford or Chevy she didn't recognize coming up their long driveway. Out of the car, on the passenger side, stepped Wes, and out of the driver's side, Mike, who was a short man, maybe 5' 3", with thick black hair and a Mediterranean complexion. She expected Mike to get back in the car, but he was making his way with Wes toward the back stairs of the house. She didn't like the intrusion and scrambled to make herself decent before they arrived at the kitchen door.

Livia said hello and asked if she could get them something to eat. Hurriedly, she took sandwich makings from the fridge. Wes said they'd been talking about a housing development that was going to be built right across the street from Mike's service station. The town board had approved it. Mike commented that he liked the open field opposite the gas station even though high school kids drank and smoked there after school and left their soda cans, beer bottles, and cigarette butts. He sometimes had one of the kids who pumped gas go and clean up the place. He said the field reminded him of the field where he and his buddies played baseball using rocks as bases before the war. Half of them were dead now, died in the Pacific. Mike had been in the Marines.

———

Twenty-six years into their marriage, she hated Wes a good deal of the time, but she had to admit there were things about him that she admired. Wes was an art lover and had a good eye for art that had not yet come into fashion but would sell for much more in a few years. They bought artwork in London at a gallery where Wes had come to know the owner, Leslie Bellingham. Wes knew that, for Bellingham, he was a minor customer compared with the truly rich. But at the same time, he believed that Bellingham genuinely liked him, appreciated his taste in art, and enjoyed doing business with him. Wes knew from his work as a life insurance broker that he took pleasure in working with some of his clients, not because they bought life insurance, but because he liked them and enjoyed talking with them.

Livia watched Bellingham teach Wes about the artists he represented — when and where they were born, whom they studied with, whose art influenced them, how critics viewed them in the past, how they view them currently, whether they've had an exhibit in New York, which galleries have shown their work in the United States and Europe. Livia felt a bit sorry for Wes as she watched him glow in Bellingham's presence. Wes spent on art only the money he'd earned, not money Livia had inherited. Over the years, he sold the paintings that had appreciated in value and bought new paintings and sculptures by other artists who were not yet in fashion. But what kept the blush on the rose, as Livia saw it, was Bellingham's acceptance of Wes as an equal in the art world, or if not an equal, a fellow art lover with a shared taste in art. Livia genuinely respected Wes for this. She had refined her own taste in art by watching him talk with Bellingham and by what Wes pointed out to her about paintings when they were in galleries and museums.

———

Neither of them was any good at sex. They'd never had any practice at it before they met. And they hadn't learned much together. They couldn't talk about it. Neither knew how to ask the other to have sex, so it was left to Wes to crawl over to Livia's adjoining twin bed to initiate sex. It ended quickly, after which he climbed back into his bed and the two of them pretended to sleep while lying quietly in the dark feeling like failures.

They had heard about the affairs other couples in their circle had had and the damage done to those marriages. Livia knew she could never have an affair, not because she thought it was disloyal, but because she was a terrible liar. She thought that men and women who have affairs don't feel sex-starved, they feel terribly lonely.

One of Livia's favorite parts of life was the train ride into the city to see her analyst, Dr. Berman. She had begun analysis to become better able to stand up to Wes regarding his harsh treatment of their older son, Stanley, who was now three. She enjoyed the train ride more than she enjoyed seeing Dr. Berman, whom she didn't particularly like. He criticized her for not being more understanding of Wes and the problems he'd had to deal with in growing up and as a soldier. Dr. Berman also thought everything was about himself. When she said she liked reading the obituaries in the *Times* each morning, he said she was looking for his name in the obituaries. The thought had never crossed her mind.

She was glad her mother had died before her own children were born. Her mother would have looked at her in a way that said in no uncertain terms: "You're a failure as a mother, just as you've been a failure at everything else you've done. Look at the husband you ended up with. And the only college that would have you was unaccredited." Her mother had gone to Barnard.

Livia liked their house in Westchester. She liked the acre of lawn in front of it and the three acres in back. During the Depression, the Civilian Conservation Corps built waist-high walls of beautifully hewn rocks through the woods along what they took to be property lines, but couldn't know for sure. There was really no need for the walls. They're beautiful in the way they stand vigil in a place where time does not exist.

On the train to and from the city, Livia slipped into a serene repose as she read *Absalom, Absalom!* a second time because she felt she hadn't understood it well enough the first time through. She'd loved reading from the time she was four years old, but she'd always felt that if anyone were to ask her what she liked about a book, she wouldn't know what to say. She could feel the differences among books she'd read, but she could never say what these differences were. She had twice read *The Mill on the Floss*. She was less interested in the characters than she was in the author, who a century ago, observed the same details of life as those that filled her own life; except of course, that Livia knew she had never fallen in love. That's not entirely true, she thought. She loved William, the younger of her two sons by two years. He was such a sweet boy. Wes didn't want much to do with William, probably because he saw how much Livia loved him. Livia was sorry she wasn't a better mother to Stanley. She'd learned with him and could be a better mother to William, she thought. Livia hadn't known what she was doing with Stanley. She had to find out for herself what it felt like to be a mother to Stanley before she could be a mother to William. On looking back on the two boys, she thought that William may have been the child she loved better, but Stanley was smarter than William. She hoped that would help carry him through life. She thought it would.

———

Wes had never cared about, nor had he been able to concentrate on, the subjects he studied in high school: Latin, French, Algebra, World History, Shakespeare, and the rest of it. His classes had one thing in common — he was bad at all of them. He couldn't memorize what the other boys could. He tried studying every free minute he had, but ultimately gave up and accepted the failing grades and withering comments dished out to him by his teachers. He had not been able to make a friend, so the days at school and the nights at home were desolate. The school allowed him to graduate out of pity, he thought. The stock market crash occurred three years before he completed high school. His father, who sold tobacco grown in Cuba to American cigar companies, lost everything.

When, at 54, Wes walked into the Academy of Art in Manhattan, it was the first time he had been inside the doors of a college. It was a stately old building with a weathered brick facade on West 52nd Street. He was nervous as he opened the door to the lobby of the building, unsure about how to conduct himself in a place he'd never imagined finding himself. He asked the secretary — an attractive woman in her 50s with faded red hair — what he had to do to audit an art history class. She was polite to him, but clearly puzzled by this request from a man more than twice the age of the students milling about in the echoes of the hallway. She spoke to him as if she were dealing with a slow man whom she wanted to treat kindly, but afraid she was only setting him up for grave disappointment. With a show of exaggerated effort to be of help, she described in detail the route he should take to get to the art history department.

As he walked the corridors, he marveled at the bulletin boards pinned with paintings, drawings, and mimeographed announcements for upcoming talks by visiting artists and evening films by Swedish and French directors he'd read about but never seen. He came upon a large room, brightly lit, in which students — the majority of whom were girls in their early 20s — engaged in different sorts of art projects. Some drew in charcoal at a rectangular table at the center of the room, others painted at easels, still others created what looked like collages, and a few at the far end of the room made open-faced boxes that reminded him of the sort of thing Joseph Cornell did with things he found on the streets of Manhattan.

Good art calmed him, excited him, and humbled him, but he knew he lacked the skill to make it. It's a kind of curse, he thought, not being able to make what he loved. They didn't teach art history or studio art at the Boys' School. Wes, unlike his older brother, Walter, had had no wish to go to college. Walter, seven years older than Wes, had gone to Penn. Wes never once visited him; their parents visited each fall and for graduation.

He walked the corridors for half an hour or so, during which he gathered himself before stepping into the corridor marked Art History Department. It was late in the afternoon. Classes had ended some time ago. He waited for a student to finish talking in the hallway with a woman who appeared to be a professor, though he couldn't be sure. She was an attractive woman, a little older than he was, with shoulder-length, thick black hair that covered a bit of her cheek on each side. Stylish, he thought.

When the conversation with the student ended, Wes introduced himself. The professor seemed startled by the sudden appearance of a handsome middle-aged man. He asked if she would give him just a minute of her time. He told her that he wondered if she might consider allowing him to audit one of her classes. She asked him which period of art he was interested in. He said it didn't matter, he just wanted to learn about the history of art. She asked if he had done any reading on his own. He told her the authors of some of the books he'd read. She asked what he thought of these books. He said that he thought they knew art history, but they didn't know art. They were dissecting art and assigning labels to periods when he had hoped they'd help him see more of the beauty in the art he sees in museums and galleries. He heard the words coming from his mouth as if someone else were speaking, someone more intelligent than he, but the words being spoken seemed right. She smiled and said that he might like to audit her class on Flemish Art. He said he would be very pleased to do that, but he didn't want to take the tests or write papers, he was no good at that, he just wanted to audit the classes. She said that was fine. He wasn't sure what to make of her. He was relieved that she hadn't asked where he'd gone to college.

Wes showed up at the time and place the professor had specified. It was mid-autumn. The semester had already begun. The students, almost all of whom were girls, were twenty or twenty-five years younger than he was. Some of them were wearing clothes that were art in their own right. One of them wore a dark green crinkly smock over black pants with a simple bright silver bracelet on her wrist. She caught him looking at her and smiled as if to her father, he thought.

—

Mike had made a habit of dropping by at lunchtime on Sundays. Lox and bagels, cream cheese, sliced onion and tomato, homemade gazpacho. Livia had initially asked Wes if he had invited Mike to lunch. He said he hadn't. He asked her if she minded. She said, no, she didn't mind, but she thought it was strange that he would invite himself to lunch. Sunday lunches had previously been a time when she and Wes talked about things that needed doing around the house: a new door-closing device on the kitchen screen door; a raise for Grace, the housekeeper, because she now, after moving apartments, drove a longer distance to their house; cancel the delivery of the *Times* while they're away.

No, she didn't mind Mike dropping by but wondered why he was doing it. Perhaps there was something about male friendship she didn't understand. Or was he after her? Or both? She had heard he'd had an affair with the wife of an actor who lives up the street, a glamorous sort of woman, not at all like the dumpy sort she is. She didn't feel like anybody's type. Sex with Wes had ceased years ago. She still felt sexually excited at times, but not in response to any man she'd met, certainly not in response to Mike. She was quiet during his Sunday visits. Mike would end each visit by jumping from his seat at the yellow Formica kitchen table saying, "Got to go. Miles to go before I sleep." What a strange thing to say, she thought. Citing a Frost poem. Does he know it's a line from a Frost poem? Probably not.

———

Waiting for one of the young gas station attendants to drive her home, Livia suddenly spun around, startled by the voice of an older man behind her. Mike laughed at her startle and said he'd drive her home. Livia felt the heat of a blush and a flash of anger cross her face. She then followed him to one of the huge cars, an old Cadillac or Imperial, parked at the side of the lot.

They drove the five minutes to the house during which they must have said something, but she couldn't remember what it was.

Mike asked if he could come in for a glass of water as if this were an ordinary request following a five-minute drive. He strode behind her up the stairs to the back door like an eager puppy following its master to the cabinet where his treats are kept. He had never been in the house when Wes wasn't there. The boys no longer lived at home and Grace was somewhere in the house.

Once inside, there was uneasy conversation about the early snow and the icy roads. Lots of accidents. More work than they can handle at the body shop. Talk about his oldest daughter who was hospitalized after another suicide attempt. A new Italian restaurant in town. Quite good. He stands to leave. Thanks her. For what, the glass of water? The taillights of the car shone brightly under the thick pewter sky as it descended the driveway. Flattered that he was flirting with her. Never had a man flirted with her. Grace, of course, curious, asked who came by. She knew perfectly well.

Mike made a practice of coming to see Livia in the ensuing months, each visit, only ten or fifteen minutes long. Talk remained superficial, though it was evident that he was there for something more than talk. Grace was in the house for most of these visits, though she stayed out of the kitchen when he was there, probably listening. Grace was a moralist and a pragmatist: disloyalty is a serious sin; people make mistakes and learn from them. Livia could just hear Grace saying this to her in her Black, Alabama drawl.

—

In the spring, Livia and Mike took short walks down the driveway and then down Krangarden Road to its end at the stone bridge where they could be alone. One day, while they stood watching the river flow over the large flat rocks in the riverbed, Mike put his hand over Livia's but kept talking as if nothing were happening. A jolt of tingling ran through her. Even though she had often imagined being touched by him, she was caught off guard by the feeling of his warm, rough skin on hers. She allowed his hand to rest there for a moment and then turned, as if interested in the call of a bird or the bark of a dog, and slid her hand out from under his. These walks were not an efficient use of his time if his intent was to seduce her, Livia thought. But she also knew that showing patience was an intelligent way to woo her.

He took pride in his cooking, he frequented restaurants on Mulberry Street in Little Italy in the city, and got on well with some of the restaurant owners there. He went on his own. He said cooking was a love of his, too personal to talk about with any but one or two close friends. Was she too personal for him to talk about with his friends, she wondered. She had been frightened by his foreignness as if the two of them were from different countries with different cultures. She had never had a friend who wasn't Jewish. His foreignness was there in the coarse texture of the skin on his hands and face, his Italian nose, his grammatical errors, and his seeming inability to feel either shame or guilt. All of this was new and very exciting.

Summer had begun. Mike waited for Livia to get out of bed and begin to dress before he got up. Awkward silence for just a moment. He told her how much he enjoyed it. She wasn't in the mood for his commentary. She was thinking about washing the sheets and about Grace who knew that she and Mike were up to something; she wasn't in the house today. Livia was absorbed in a conversation with herself. Given the fact that the affair had begun, she and Wes were now in an entirely different relationship. She'd never had a secret from him of this magnitude during the twenty-four years they'd been married. She'd never, so far as she could remember, succeeded in deceiving him or anyone else. Mike had dressed. What am I supposed to say to him, she wondered. They'd used the bed in William's room. It had felt strange sleeping with Mike in the bed William, their younger son, still slept it when he visited.

———

Wes had told Livia he was attending art history classes at the New York Academy of Arts. She suspected he was having flirtations with girls in his classes, or with his teachers, and some of these flirtations may become affairs or may already be affairs, though she doubted it. The idea that he was having affairs would never have occurred to her before she'd begun hers. Wes was dressing more stylishly. He had bought new suits, new ties, new shoes. All tasteful, she thought. Comparing Wes and Mike was laughable. Wes was far better looking, but she didn't love him, didn't even like him much. Mike unsuccessfully attempted Italian high style with dirt under his fingernails.

One evening in early autumn the following year, Livia was stunned when it came time for bed. She had not heard Wes using the bathroom after her, as was his habit. The two of them had had supper together, though Wes didn't eat much, as was also his habit. She looked in the living room and upstairs and then called his name into the dark cellar. She worried something had happened to him, perhaps a heart attack. Only on going into the kitchen did she notice the lights on in the Little House across the patio. She couldn't see him from where she stood, nor could she detect any flickering of light that would indicate someone was in there. On returning to the bathroom, she saw that he had removed his toothbrush and electric shaver, and on checking his closet, she saw that he had removed several shirts, suits, and shoes.

Livia wondered if he had learned of her affair. As far as she knew, only one person other than Mike knew of the affair, and that was Grace. But lots of people could have suspected: neighbors or friends driving by might have noticed a car parked in the driveway that they knew wasn't Wes's or hers; some of the men working for Mike might have noticed his repeated absences; Mike's wife may have sensed something, though an affair would not have been new to her.

As she sat in the darkened kitchen, she knew that an irreversible change had occurred, and she didn't like it. She had planned on living with Wes and sleeping with Mike, at least for a while, perhaps for years. She didn't want a divorce, she liked being married, she liked their house, she liked living where she and Wes had raised their children, the house where her friends came to talk or go swimming in their pool in the summer. She didn't know what Wes had in mind about having their meals together, handling their money, repairing the house, going on vacation, or making plans about anything. Are they to be a couple in any sense of the word?

What she liked least was that all of this was up to him. He'd tell her how it would be. Not by means of a conversation — which is a medium of communication in which he rarely engaged — but by means of what he chooses to do. Will they share the kitchen, the refrigerator, the automatic coffee pot? She would have to wait to find out what he wanted, and she didn't like that one bit. She had squandered more than she'd realized. At that moment, standing in the kitchen, looking at the quietly illuminated Little House, she thought, I like Mike, and I like being liked by Mike, but I could never get myself to believe I love him. I have loved two people in my life, Stanley and William, so I know what love feels like. I also know I have never been in love, and most likely never will be.

———

The house in which Wes had lived with Livia now felt cold to him. He felt no connection with the piano he once played. The artwork on the walls felt like a museum exhibit he had no interest in seeing. He rarely had a meal with Livia, and when he did, the two of them had strained conversations. Wes could not remember ever feeling sexually attracted to Livia, which made him wonder why he married her, before reminding himself of the state he was in when he gave Livia 48 hours to accept or reject his proposal of marriage. He thought she was not unattractive, pretty at times, but certainly not beautiful. Given the way he'd felt about himself when he was young, beautiful wasn't in the cards for him. He knew he was going to be drafted and wanted a wife at home waiting for him.

He felt handsome now for the first time in his life. Till now, his older brother Walter was the handsome one. People had told Wes, as a child and as a teenager, that he too was handsome, but he always thought that they were straining to find something charitable to say to him.

The Flemish Art History class at the Academy was the place where he first felt handsome. Louise Freeman, the professor, and the female students seemed drawn to him in a way he hadn't expected and had never experienced. And for reasons he couldn't understand, he was able to reinvent himself. This felt miraculous to him. He was too old to be a brother, but not too young to be a father to the students in the class. At first, he'd been unsteady with the students in the Flemish art history class. He had tried to be charming, tried to smile naturally, and then realized that when he stopped trying, he could enjoy being with them, some of whom were very pretty, and loved art as much as he did. At times he felt like Fred Astaire: dapper, always with a smile about to bloom, polite, deferential to the opposite sex. Wes, like Fred Astaire, liked girls, not in preparation for having sex with them, but because he liked the way they talked and moved and laughed and thought, which he could see was what melted their hearts. Where did that come from? He had always thought that girls were his brother Walter's domain: Walter, who would affectionately ruffle Wes's hair and say, "Ya' know, you're not as dumb as ya' look."

Louise Freeman somehow made it clear to the girls that she had first dibs on Wes, though she would never have admitted that to anyone, perhaps not even to herself. She invited him to lunch in the Faculty Dining Room. He could tell she was impressed by his knowledge of art, the way he talked about a Bonnard painting in a current exhibit at the Met or a Modigliani sculpture at the MOMA. Wes felt Louise was too old for him, but he didn't want to hurt her feelings. She'd given him his first opportunity to attend an art history class, and he was grateful to her for that. He felt as if she'd released him from the mundane — being a husband, a father, an insurance broker — and had invited him into the world in which the principal questions were, What makes this work of art beautiful or powerful or comical or ironic or mysterious?

———

They'd been living separately for years now — he in the Little House, she across the patio — their lives overlapping, but nothing more. She missed sleeping next to someone. She missed having an ordinary life. No one knew of the new arrangements with Wes and with Mike. No one except Grace. Livia didn't have secrets, she was living a secret.

Wes had been pressing Livia to cut Grace's time. She reluctantly agreed to tell her that there was much less to do — now that the boys were out of the house and rarely visited and Wes was living in the Little House — so they'd like her to come three days a week instead of four. When, as they ate lunch together in the kitchen, Livia told Grace about the new arrangement, Grace fumed and then stormed out of the kitchen. She returned a few minutes later saying that she couldn't pay the electric bill if she was working less, so she was going to look for another job. Livia tried to calm her, but Grace would have none of it.

What Livia hadn't fully understood, and hadn't fully reciprocated, was Grace's feeling that she was a member of the family and a friend of Livia's. Grace and Livia had had lunch together on the days Grace worked. They'd talked of their worries about their children and about the March on Washington in which Grace had participated, and the speech she'd heard Martin Luther King deliver during the march. And they even talked about the affair and the possibility that Wes or the boys would suspect something. Grace had sometimes prepared lunch for Livia and Mike. She was the only person who Livia could talk with about the affair; Livia was the only person Grace could talk with about one of her sons serving time in state prison in Upstate New York for armed robbery. It was true that Livia had stopped thinking of Grace as a maid. But she wasn't a friend, she was just Grace. When she thought about it, she saw that she'd been deluding herself. She'd kept out of mind the fact that Grace was a Black woman in her 50s who lived with her husband in a tiny flat. Livia had tried to disguise Grace's poverty by giving her a reliable car — she couldn't bear watching Grace get out of her wreck of a car. She also gave Grace generous checks for her birthday and Christmas. But that didn't make her a friend.

They could have afforded to continue having Grace come four days a week. It was true that the boys had been out of the house for years, but you don't tell a friend or member of the family they're not needed as much, so they should visit less.

The glare in Grace's eyes as she stared at Livia that day would never leave Livia's memory. The next day, Grace asked if "the Missus" had time to talk with her. They sat across the kitchen table from one another.

"I never felt so kicked in the teeth as when you said you were going to cut me back to three days. You act like I'm just like every other Negro woman working for a white lady, and the white woman can just tell you you're not needed. Who am I fooling all these years? I thought you weren't just a boss to me."

Livia didn't like being confronted by Grace. She listened patiently. When Grace finished saying what she had to say, Livia said that she did feel Grace was a part of the family, but she had to have the right to make decisions about how much time was needed to keep the house as Grace has been keeping it. She knew that saying this to Grace would hurt her and that things would never be the same. For the rest of her life, Livia felt ashamed of how she'd treated Grace that day.

——

Livia's life seemed now a network of affairs. Wes made no secret of the fact he was taking one of his "little sweeties" — as Livia called them — to Philadelphia to see the Barnes, or flying to Boston to see the Gardner, or to D.C. to see the Hirschhorn. They never stayed overnight. Livia didn't know why these excursions should make her feel jealous, but they did.

Mike told Livia he'd had affairs with two other women, each affair lasting for years. He didn't mention their names, but Livia knew who they were. She told herself she didn't care. Her affair had gone on for several years now. She asked herself how this part of her life would have felt to her without the affair. Probably very lonely.

Livia felt little admiration for either Wes or Mike. That's a sad thing to say about the men in her life, she thought. She knew she was comparing them with her father who had been the president of the large family company and carried himself with a type of dignity that may have died with his generation.

——

Livia told Stanley that his father had moved to the Little House. He'd been aware that there was trouble between them, but now it was out in the open.

His father had always been quiet, but now and again he'd tell Stanley something about himself or about how he saw Stanley. These talks came about like shooting stars — there for an instant, and then gone. Stanley could remember not only what his father had said at those times, but he could remember exactly where they were when he made those observations about himself or about life. These observations included only one piece of advice: "Don't ever work for anybody." Stanley was 16 or 17 at the time. Vivid in Stanley's memory was the fact that his father wasn't looking at him as he said this and acted as if he hadn't said anything.

When Stanley was a little older, as they were standing on the roof of the first story of the house, putting up storm windows, his father had said something that sounded as if he were picking up on a conversation they'd had hours or days or weeks before. He told him that he had liked Franz Bauer, the father of his friend Peter. Franz was born in Germany and immigrated here in his 20s, his father said. He designed wallpaper and sold it in an exclusive shop in New York. He and Franz had shared a love of art. His father said that he'd felt that he and Franz were good friends, but Franz stopped returning his calls, which his father took to be Franz's way of telling him that he was not as intelligent and sophisticated as Franz expected of a friend. He remembered his father going on working on the storm windows, not asking for a reply to what he'd said. Telling Stanley seemed to be all he'd wanted.

Stanley could recall his father talking to him about his family as he grew up. He was driving Stanley to the station to take a train back to college after the Easter break. His father said to him, "You know that something's gotten in the way of my being a father to you. I'm proud of you, but what gets in the way is that you're so much like my brother. Things come easy to you and Henry, but most things don't come easy to me. He did well at sports and at school, and he was good with the girls. He went to dance halls. I didn't."

Stanley remembered replying that things may seem like they come easy to him, but that's not the way it feels. He had to work very hard to achieve what he did. His father seemed to think about what he'd said but didn't say anything in response.

———

Not long after telling Grace that she was cutting her hours, it seemed to Livia that Grace was threatening to tell Wes about the affair. This may or may not have been the case, but Livia decided to tell Wes herself.

Livia and Wes were in the kitchen one Sunday talking about household business when she said, "I want to tell you something, so it comes from me and not from someone else." Wes interrupted her. "I know about the affair with Mike. I've known about it all along." He told her he had had affairs with girls from the Art Institute, the ones who'd gone on trips with him to art museums in other cities. Livia didn't believe it. She thought he was just saving face. Her telling Wes marked the end of the affair with Mike, and she told this to Wes, though that didn't seem to matter to him.

———

For most of a decade, after Livia ended her affair with Mike, she and Wes lived amicably, though not warmly, across the patio from one another, she in the big house, he in the Little House. It came as a shock to her when Stanley called her to let her know that Wes had been admitted to Lenox Hill Hospital. Stanley explained that Wes had called him just ten minutes earlier at his law firm and spoke to him as if this might be the last time they'd ever speak to one another. Stanley told Wes he'd let Livia and William know. Livia had last seen Wes a week earlier as he left the Little House and walked to his car in the garage. She'd thought he looked thinner, but she hadn't made much of it. She hadn't really looked at him. Rarely did.

Livia was quite agitated as she drove to the city, almost hitting a car as she changed lanes without looking. She didn't know if Wes had had an accident or was ill, but Wes wouldn't have spoken to Stanley in the way he had if it were something minor.

After thumbing through a sheaf of papers looking for Wes's name, the woman at the hospital reception desk gave Livia directions to his room. Livia took the elevator to the third floor in the South Wing and made her way down the pale green hallway, watching the numbers go by — 312, 314, 316 — each with an oversized wooden door and a 6' x 6' window to its right. Her mind was blank, simply counting. 318, Wes's name on the chart next to the door. Through the window she saw Wes in the bed, his upper body slightly elevated. A woman, seated on the plastic-coated orange cushion of the armchair next to the bed, had her hand on his as she talked. He looked weak. Did that woman really believe that she was the one to be taking care of him? As absurd as it was, and she knew it was ridiculous, she had till now firmly believed that the "till death do us part" segment of their wedding vows continued to be a binding commitment that gave her the right to the chair next to his bed. She realized in that moment, as she looked into his room, that she had not only lost that right, she may have lost the right even to be a visitor.

The woman next to his bed was dressed informally, but tastefully. She wore her blond hair in a perfect pixie haircut, a cut too young for her, Livia thought. She was cute and knew it. The woman was more than a decade younger than Wes, possibly twenty years, maybe twenty-five. Of course, that's what a man his age wants. The woman held his hand in a way that staked her claim to him. Livia knew she could be inventing a story about this woman who may only be a colleague or a friend, but she doubted it. Livia's legs weakened. Not to make a fool of herself by collapsing at the window, she slowly, deliberately made her way back to the small waiting room with its plastic potted palm opposite the elevator.

Sitting there, she tried to think rationally. She didn't know anything about the woman. She may be jumping to conclusions. The woman could be a friend. Maybe one of his sweethearts from his art history classes is taking care of an old man who reminds her of her father. Sixty-three seems ancient for a woman in her thirties or early 40s. Her mother had said that "old" is ten years beyond your own age. He looked exhausted as he lay there, his face looking up at the ceiling, his eyes barely open.

"Wes may not have the energy to resist the woman's help. We've been married for thirty-six years," Lydia said to herself. "We're having a difficult time now, and have for a long time, but neither of us has ever used the word divorce. I've never wanted a divorce. I had Mike, and Wes has had his sweeties, but we're still married, we still are the parents of Stanley and William, and we still live together in our own way. He called Stanley and not me. That's too small a detail to dwell on."

Livia didn't want to go into the room while the woman was there. She didn't know if the woman would ever leave but she refused to go home without seeing him.

As Livia pushed open the door, the woman startled. She was a girl, just a girl, a pretty girl, who now looked to be in her mid-thirties. Wes opened his eyes, saying Livia's name as if naming an item on a shelf to demonstrate that his memory hadn't failed him.

"Wes, how are you?"

Wes looked at her blankly.

"I was worried by Stanley's phone call," she said, refusing to acknowledge the presence of the woman in the chair who probably had not yet been born when she and Wes married.

"Yes, I was going to call you, but I was too tired."

Livia began to say something when the woman interrupted her. "Livia, I'm Chloe."

Livia was surprised by the fact the woman knew who she was when she hadn't known this woman existed.

"Who are you?"

"I'm with Wes."

"Apparently so. But who are you?"

"I'm Chloe Brandt, Wes and I are together," she said in a firm, steady voice. "You may not know this, you probably don't, but Wes and I live together with our two daughters, 5 and 3."

"Children?"

"They're ours, Wes's and mine."

"That can't be so."

Livia felt her mother looking at her in a way that made it clear that she had failed as a woman and wife in the worst possible way, just as she'd failed as a child. She'd blinded herself to what would have been readily apparent to anyone with the least bit of intelligence. She could not reconfigure the world in the few seconds during which these facts were pouring in. Wes was silent, face to the ceiling, eyes shut. Chloe is tough, calm, and poised as she sits there. She must have prepared for this moment, writing the script for it over and over in her mind.

"Wes, would you tell me why you're here in the hospital?"

"I have acute lymphocytic leukemia." He hardly had the energy to say these words.

"How bad is that?"

"It's bad."

Livia didn't know what to say.

"I'm tired, very tired."

"How long have you known?"

"A couple of months."

Livia wiped tears from her cheeks with the backs of her hands. She turned to Chole. "Would you let me have a little while with Wes by ourselves?"

Chloe asked Wes if that was all right with him. He nodded.

After Chloe left the room, Livia remained standing, not wanting to sit in Chloe's chair. She couldn't quite believe that Wes had another family.

"Wes, is it true?"

He looked at her and said, "It is."

"You don't live there with her, do you?"

"I do a lot of the time."

"How can that be? You live in the Little House, don't you?"

"I don't have the energy to spell it out."

"You sleep in the Little House sometimes?"

"Sometimes."

How stupid I've been, she thought, for wanting to believe he's been in the Little House every night and that he drove to the train station in the morning before I've awoken.

Though she was tempted to let fury fly, she couldn't do that to him as he lay there in a hospital bed.

On walking back into the hallway, she saw Chloe leaning against the wall opposite Wes's room pretending not to see her leaving.

On arriving home, Livia sat on the raspberry couch in the living room, which looked different from the way she remembered it. The living room had once been their living room, the room in which they did a good part of their living, the living room in which Wes had said to the woman selling the house, "This Jew's going to buy it." The room where Wes read a chapter of *Charlotte's Web* to the boys each night, at the end of which William wept such big wet tears and Stanley was choked up. What's happened to that family?

———

Livia called Stanley on the evening of her visit to Wes at the hospital. After she told him about his father's other family, he said,

"So our family was of such little importance to him that he just threw us away and made a new family for himself. He cashed the three of us in and got himself a new young wife and two new children. Why didn't he ask for a divorce? He kept a tie to us in a way that feels cowardly to me."

Livia felt renewed rage as she listened to Stanley.

Stanley said he couldn't get himself to believe his father was on his deathbed. "I haven't seen him in months. We talk on the phone most every week. I've been afraid for a long time that I'm like him, as self-preoccupied as he is. I put myself first with girlfriends. When I'm working, no one exists; even I don't exist."

Livia asked Stanley not to talk with William until she spoke to him the next day. She wanted to be the one to tell him. She was too exhausted to call him now. The following morning, when she told William about his father's other family, William said that, at first, he thought she was talking about someone else's father with two families. "I didn't count for much to him. Maybe he found me cute when I was little, but then he lost interest in me. I don't think he was much interested in Stanley either, though he was more competitive with him, so Stanley did matter to him in that way."

"I don't think what you're saying is true. Dad liked doing things with you. When he was less preoccupied, he'd play with you, not with Stanley. Dad liked doing things with you. I thought you both liked it when you helped him with barbecuing."

"That's pretty thin evidence that I mattered to him, don't you think?"

———

Wes was bone-weary. It was a great effort for him even to roll over in bed. He would tell himself he was going to roll over in five minutes, and he'd gather himself for it, but it took him an hour or more before he'd be able to do it.

And all the rancor between Livia and Chloe felt unnecessary to him. If he'd had the energy, he would have liked to say to them, "I don't know why you can't just think of it as a fact that doesn't need to be squabbled over. Please, just let it be." He felt he hadn't gotten involved with Chloe to get back at Livia for her affair. "I don't know why I wanted two homes," he said to himself. "That's just the way it was. I've gone to such lengths not to hurt Livia and the boys.

I don't want people around me fighting now. I'm not afraid of dying, I'd just like to do it in peace."

———

Livia wasn't with Wes when he died. He'd been discharged from Lennox Hill Hospital into hospice care at the house where he lived with Chloe. That was the place that felt like home to him, Livia supposed. Wes didn't want Livia or the boys to visit him there. He preferred to talk by phone.

Chloe seemed relieved not to have to take part in planning Wes's funeral. Livia arranged to hold the funeral service at Temple Israel in the city, the temple her parents and Wes's parents belonged to. Though the preparations for the funeral were not difficult for Livia, the funeral itself was hell. When she arrived at the Synagogue two hours before the service, Chloe and her two little girls were already there. They'd camped in the front row on one side of the aisle. Livia, Stanley, and William took seats in the front row on the other side.

Several days earlier, the rabbi had asked Livia for the names of people who might want to speak at the service. There were friends, from the insurance agency — Big and Little Harry — whom Wes liked very much; Vivian, the office manager with whom he often went to lunch; and Charlie Drimmel, who ran the agency. Franz Bauer told Livia that something had gone wrong between him and Wes, but he'd like to say a few words at the service. Livia hadn't asked Chloe for names of people she'd like to invite to speak. It was small of her, she knew. As people arrived for the service, it was clear that there was tension between those who knew Wes as part of his family with Livia, and those who knew him as part of his family with Chloe.

When the hundred-and-fifty or so people were seated, the room hushed as the organ began making doleful sounds. It was gratifying to Livia that there were empty seats on Chloe's side of the aisle, while her side was flush with their friends. Rabbi Adler conducted the funeral in a relaxed fashion, welcoming everyone there to remember Wes. He'd known both Livia's parents and Wes's. He remembered Wes as frail when he was a child. There was some singing and praying before the speakers took their turns. They'd been told to keep what they said to five minutes. The speakers had amusing stories about Wes's idiosyncratic ways. Vivian spoke about Wes's attention to the way he dressed, and how he wore very fashionable clothes and paid particular attention to his shoes, which he once confided, were hand-made for him at a shop in London. There were warm chuckles from Livia's side of the aisle in response to Vivian's description of Wes, and dead silence from the other side where the guests seemed not to recognize this depiction of him. They understood even less of Franz Bauer's speaking of Wes's deep appreciation of art and his fine eye for what was truly original in a painting or sculpture.

After Livia and Wes's friends had spoken, it came as a surprise to Livia that a man whom she did not recognize stepped up to the dais. Almost as a retort to what had been said by the previous speakers, he talked about Wes's relaxed, accepting ways, his never allowing anger to guide him, and told stories about his deep love of his little girls and his devotion to Chloe. None of the previous speakers had mentioned either Wes's devotion to Livia or the fact he had two sons. Livia realized she had underestimated Chloe.

———

"I'd like to get together with you to talk," Livia said, finally getting the nerve to call. Chloe said that she'd have to think about it and brought the phone call to an abrupt end.

A month later, Chloe called saying that she'd like to invite Livia over for a cup of tea. Livia thought the idea of their having tea together was a bit too precious. She agreed to the visit but was wary of being ambushed. Their house was in a marginal part of Mount Vernon. From the outside, the house was as typically suburban as one can get — a modest ranch house with a small, ill-kept lawn that was not much different from the other houses running down both sides of the street.

Chloe was dressed in a silk blouse and pleated skirt. She was a pretty woman, Livia had to admit, but she seemed like an ice queen, very practiced in her manner. Livia followed Chloe into the kitchen where there was a plate of uninviting Pepperidge Farm cookies on the kitchen table. Chloe turned on the flame under a rather beat-up tea kettle.

"You're probably shocked that Wes bought a place like this for us."

"I vowed to myself that I'd speak only what I feel to be true today, which is rather the rule for me. I call myself pathologically honest, which has lost me quite a number of friends over the years. So, I'll tell you the truth. I expected your house to be pretty much as it is — functional and unpretentious. Wes hated my snobbery and just wanted a place to live where he felt comfortable."

"I've seen your house and I wouldn't trade places with you."

"All right, now that that's out of the way, tell me why you changed your mind about talking with me."

"I changed my mind because I want the girls, Ariel and Susie, to get to know members of the family that you and Wes made. I am out of touch with my parents and brother, and I want the girls to have William and Stanley as half-brothers and whatever other aunts and uncles and cousins there may be."

"I can't speak for William and Stanley, but they're kind men, and I'd imagine they'd like to get to know their half-sisters. You haven't said what role you'd like me to play."

"I haven't said because I don't know. I don't know what kind of person you'd be to the girls."

"So, I'm on audition. I don't blame you for that. I'd do the same, but not as well as you're doing it."

"I suppose that's one way of putting it. I'd prefer to say that we're getting to know one another."

After they talked for another half-hour, Chloe called the girls from their rooms and introduced Livia to them. "Livia was a close friend of Daddy's."

— Fathers and Sons —

At the corner of Vallejo and San Fernando Streets in Boyes Hot Springs, men are standing on the sidewalk waiting for work. I pull up a few yards and stop. Four men lunge in front of the others and pull open the back door of the car trying to pile into the back seat. Two push past the others and grab a seat. A third squeezes in next to them. I say, "Just two." The third sheepishly gets out of the car.

Before pulling out, I tell them the hourly pay. One nods, I don't know if the other man speaks enough English to understand what I've said. The one who nodded has a young face, his beard hardly more than that of an adolescent. We wait at a stoplight in silence. After a couple of minutes, my eyes fixed on the street ahead, I say, "I'm Raymond," as if that matters to either of them. I assume they are undocumented, so I doubt they'd give me real names. I read in the local paper that a month ago the INS raided Boyes Hot Springs and took four men into detention, leaving a chill in the air. The men in the back give the names, "Phillipe," the younger one, and "Mateo." Nothing more is said until we arrive. The house stands 50 yards up the side of a dry grassy hill punctuated by bay trees and a madrone growing out of the stump of a felled oak.

Phillipe and Mateo stand next to the car looking first at the house and then down the hill toward the main road. Phillipe appears to be in his early 20s, his long black hair tied in a bun at the back, his body gaunt, but hard. Mateo is a tall, grizzled man in his 40s wearing a faded T-shirt the color of Dijon mustard, and black work boots missing the tongue on one foot. He walks with a swagger that announces he can be hired but he can't be bought. I wonder if he thinks I've proposed buying him. It's getting warm. The morning has already shed its coat of the night's cool air.

"I need help painting the house. I have the paint." I don't know if they understand, and I suspect they'd like to keep it that way.

Mateo, the elder of the two, turns his head toward me as if to say, Just tell us what you want us to do, then leave us alone and we'll do it.

I lead the way along a dirt path to the gambrel-roofed barn, once a working shelter for farm machinery, which I now use only for storage. As I throw the switch just to the right of the door to turn on the lights, mice scurry across the concrete floor toward the dark corners. Stepping around areas of bat droppings, I stoop to pick up two new cans of paint I'd put away a week ago, mouse droppings on the metal tops.

Phillipe asks in a thick Mexican accent, "What do you want us to paint?"

"We'll work on a side of the house."

"There?" he asks, pointing back to the house. I'm aware these men depend on well-off people like me for money to pay for food, clothing, and shelter. What for me is a chore, for them is a necessity, a means of survival. It is not lost to me that while I'm offering them money for an honest day's work, I'm paying them far less than I'd pay a professional painter and I'm offering no benefits. Admittedly, they are utterly untrained.

For the rest of the day, on ladders, we sweep dirt and cobwebs out of the way, sand, and apply primer. Mateo talks with Phillipe in Spanish. They shoot glances at one another when I point to places that need more sanding or another coat of primer. One of them brought a radio, perhaps in a satchel I hadn't noticed. Phillipe places the radio next to him, an old portable model splattered with paint, which he tunes to a Spanish music station and turns it up loud. I can hear nothing but the thin, raspy sound of a man singing backed by a band that seems to be composed exclusively of trumpets and guitars. He clearly doesn't like working side by side with a *gringo* boss and plays his music defiantly loud to make sure I know how he feels. The last thing I want to do is antagonize this man who is much bigger and stronger than I am. For about half an hour, I restrain myself from asking him to turn it down. When I finally ask, he gives me a puzzled look.

I'm certain he knows exactly what I'm asking. He turns the music down to a volume less punishing, but far from pleasant. The day stretches into late afternoon. A good deal of work has been done but it is by no means complete. We gather up the canvas drop cloths and carry them to a corner of the garage where we fold and stack them.

While driving the men back to the corner where I picked them up, I ask Mateo for his phone number, saying that I'd like to have him back to work another weekend. I have no compunction about ignoring Phillipe. I fish out of the glove compartment a pencil and pad for him to write down a phone number. I don't know if he wants to be called, but he writes something down.

—

A couple of weeks later, I arrive at the pick-up point mid-morning to find no one waiting for work. The sidewalk, once filled with men talking to one another in Spanish, now is as quiet as a sports arena in the off-season. I try the phone numbers of two men only to find that the numbers are not in use. I try calling the number Mateo gave me. A man with a thick Hispanic accent answers. I ask if Mateo is there.

"Mateo doesn't stay here," the man says.

"Do you know where I can find him?"

"No."

I pause and then ask, "By any chance would you like to work today?"

"Yes," he says quietly.

"Where can I pick you up?"

"McDonald's. Solano Avenue. You know?"

"Yes, I know it. Can you be there in half an hour?"

On arriving at the McDonald's, I look around the parking lot and see a man in his early- to mid-40s standing in the back of the restaurant.

"Raymond," I say, putting out my hand.

"Armando." His hand is large and rough. He grips my hand loosely. His shirt is large for him as if he's lost weight recently. The skin on his face is deeply rutted from working for years in the sun, I presume. He has a calm, composed manner about him.

"There," he says, pointing to the area of the parking lot behind the restaurant near the trash cans. At first, I think he's telling me there's another worker there who wants to work with him. He takes a few steps in that direction and points to a van, a beat-up thing with faded green paint and a multitude of dents. I'm surprised that he owns a van or drives someone else's van. This, too, makes me feel I'm meeting someone different from the other laborers I've hired.

His face is weathered, but the most remarkable feature of his face is his soft brown eyes. He is wearing old work pants, the zipper torn, the waist several sizes too big, a rope strung through belt loops.

There is weeding to be done on a couple of acres of downward sloping land waist-high with thistles and long dry grass. There's also an overgrown, parched lavender garden to the side of the house that needs tending. Crawling on hands and knees, Armando and I reach under the thorny leaves of the thistles to get to the roots of the plants. All around us stand groups of three-foot-tall thistles.

Armando seems to know as little about gardening as I do. He is careful and deliberate in his ways. He moves and talks quietly and communicates by using a few English words and sentence fragments. We talk primarily by hand movement.

It's a hot cloudless day with a dazzling, deep blue sky. We stuff the weeds into four-feet-deep cylindrical canvas baskets that we empty onto the compost heap at the top of the hill. Armando's gloves are old, with a large hole at the end of each finger. I have no extra gloves to lend him. We work together silently. Every hour or so we take a break and a drink in the shade from bottles of water, quiet not because we didn't have anything to say, but because we didn't know how to say it.

After working for about four hours, we gather our baskets and tools and return to the garage where we put the tools back. I ask Armando what I should pay him. He signals that it's up to me. I pay him and ask if he's free to work next week at the same time. At first, he doesn't understand. After I repeat my question, he says, "No Saturday. Sunday okay. Same time?"

I nod and we shake hands.

I stand there on the driveway as he gets into his van. He sits there for a while. I eventually realize he doesn't want to start the van while I'm watching. I imagine he has trouble starting it and doesn't want me watching him struggle with his van.

The following Sunday morning, I wait on the driveway in the cool air listening to the chatter of blue jays until I hear Armando's van laboriously making its way up the steep driveway. He parks about twenty yards from me. I'm surprised that two people step out of the van. As the passenger walks around the far side of the van, I see that he is a child, a boy with broad shoulders.

"Junior," Armando says, looking down at the boy standing close to his father.

"Yes, glad to meet you," I say putting my hand out to the boy. "Do they call you 'junior' at school?"

"No, they call me Armando," he says in a clear voice with a Mexican accent.

"Since your father is here, may I call you Armandito?" He smiles and nods, delighted I know enough Spanish to call him by the diminutive. He's about ten, with a round face and bright eyes which give him the appearance of a cherub. He's a sweet boy.

The three of us crawl in parallel paths as we pull thistles and push them into canvas bags. I've bought extra pairs of gardening gloves that I give to Armando and his son. While I'm working, the universe is the square yard on which I'm pulling thistles, a wretched spiked weed with tiny yellow flowers, each of which will create seeds that will float in the breeze to new soil in which to take root. I know very little about gardening, though I've taught myself something about drip system irrigation.

The next Sunday, I hear Armando driving his van slowly up the hill to the house at 9:00 A.M., as we'd agreed. Armando and Armandito slowly step down from opposite sides of the van exchanging a few words in Spanish. Armando has a blue bandana wrapped around his forehead to keep sweat from dripping into his eyes as he works. Armandito is a cute boy, a little chubby in a way that makes me want to hug him.

"Is this yours?" Armandito asks as he looks up the hill behind the house that disappears into a forest of oaks and redwoods.

"I live here, but it's not really mine. I've borrowed it. You give back everything you have when you die."

"You think that?"

"Don't you?" I ask.

"I don't know. I just believe some things."

"What do you believe?"

"Things my father tells me."

I ask, "Would you mind if I ask what your father says?"

"He says you should be honest. You should work hard. You should look after your family."

It is by now clear why Armando has brought his son. Armandito, who speaks English quite well, serves as a translator for his father who speaks only a few words of English, though he understands more than he's able to speak. But it occurs to me that Armando is not bringing his son simply to be his translator, he's bringing him to improve his English by talking with me, and perhaps learn something more.

———

There is no landline in the house and the signal for my mobile phone is weak, but I don't mind. There is little in life that I value more than a quiet place to live. In my childhood, peace was hard to find. Most every night at the dinner table, our father, who was a political science professor, would pose to my older brother, Arthur, questions such as, Do you think it is just to tax a person's wealth in addition to taxing his income? Should college admission standards be lowered for minorities? How does art differ from craft? Long exchanges followed in which Walter (Arthur and I called our father Walter behind his back) would deftly counter each point Arthur made until it was clear that Arthur had been defeated. Our mother and I just listened because we were not deemed qualified to take part. Though we were felt to be insufficiently intelligent to understand the questions being discussed, we could serve as an audience for the event.

After Arthur and I cleared the dishes from the dinner table, swept the floor, and brought out the garbage, we would leave the kitchen trying not to catch Walter's attention. We'd walk silently up the stairs and down the hall to Arthur's room where we talked about the way Walter had cast himself in the role of Socrates. As much as Arthur was pained by the duel with Walter, I knew he took pride in being deemed worthy to be the opponent with whom Walter jousted. As time went on, Arthur became exhausted by the contests, but he could not deny Walter the pleasure of the ritual.

I begged Arthur not to accept the invitation Walter issued him to debate. But Arthur couldn't let go of what he thought was Walter's affection for him. In retrospect, it's easy to see that Walter was a fragile man who needed to feel he had some strength — actually, heroic strength — at a time when his marriage was failing and his standing in his department at the university was in decline.

Arthur devoted himself to his studies in high school. He labored deep into the night and allowed himself only Saturday night off to watch television. He fought fiercely to achieve the grades necessary to get into a prestigious university. When Arthur applied to the university Walter had attended, Walter refused to write a letter of recommendation for him because he felt that Arthur wasn't qualified to attend. Arthur was accepted by that university but chose to go elsewhere. This was one of his few acts of defiance against Walter.

Arthur struggled in college. He'd call me wanting to talk about how lonely he felt. He said he had no friends and was frightened to go to class. He told me that he was unable to touch his dirty clothes, particularly his underwear, so his clothes lay in a pile at the foot of his bed. At the end of freshman year, he was placed on academic probation and told to take a year off before reapplying for admission.

During the year that followed, Arthur lived at home. He took courses at the local junior college where he knew no one, which suited him. He told me he felt freer to think at the junior college because it was a school Walter would never deign to attend. "He wouldn't have set foot in the place. It's a place for people who can't make it at a real college. I belong there."

———

"You can't get all the thistles. Some'll be back next year," I say to Armandito who isn't listening to me because he's having trouble getting on the oversized work gloves I'd given him. We walk to the edge of the field where I show him how to pull up weeds at the root, which interests him, I imagine because he wants to be able to do everything his father does. Today is a hot day, over 100 degrees, which depletes Armandito and me, but not Armando who insists on carrying up the hill to the compost heap the canvas baskets the three of us fill. After a couple of hours, I tell them I'd like help with the lavender garden near the house. Armandito translates for his father in so few words that I suspect he's editing out the parts that he doesn't think are important enough to repeat.

"What kind of work does your father do?" I ask Armandito as if his father weren't there. As soon as the question leaves my lips, I'm embarrassed by what I've done.

"A concrete company," Armandito tells me.

Armando turns his head on hearing the word "concrete" and says something to me in Spanish, which Armandito translates: "He makes wooden frames, he spreads the concrete as it's poured into the frames for foundations for houses and sidewalks and other things. Starts at five in hot weather, like today." Armando nods.

They follow me into the garage, where I show them a hundred-foot coil of half-inch black rubber tubing I've stored under the makeshift workbench — planks of wood atop stacked cinder blocks at each end. I show the coil to Armando hoping he'll tell me if he's ever used this kind of tubing. He takes the coil and says, "Where?" I don't know if this means he's familiar with installing drip-line irrigation or if it means he's willing to try anything. We go to the lavender garden at the side of the house which I've been hand-watering. I open my toolbox containing plastic emitters, splices, hole plugs, and a hole puncher. Armando stares into the box preparing to figure out how these things work.

The three of us walk out to the lavender garden in which about twenty-five French lavender plants are wilting. I take the coil of half-inch black tubing from Armando and begin to lay it down. I motion to Armando to secure it with two-pronged metal stakes as I go. Before we've laid a yard of tubing, Armando takes the coil from me and lifts it to his shoulder. He says something to Armandito before putting the boy's right arm through the center of the coil of tubing, signaling him to lay it down as he uses metal hooks to secure the tubing.

At the end of each row, Armandito gently curves the tubing so that it bends, without a crimp. Armando moves like an agile bear as he pushes the metal hooks into the earth; Armandito moves like a cat as he lays down the tubing. I later explain how to punch holes in the half-inch tubing and insert various connectors and emitters.

Armando refuses to be the one to decide when we should stop working. He leaves that entirely to me. When I say we've done enough for the day, they pack up the tubing, emitters, spikes, and the rest of it, while I run into the house to get money to pay them. I pay Armandito half of what I pay his father but give all the pay to Armando.

Armandito's a boy overbrimming with enthusiasm, an intelligent boy, a boy hungry to learn and grow up and become a man like his father. He quickly learns to piece together the drip system as well as his father and I can, and when his father's hands are too big to get into a space where we've dropped an emitter or connector, Armandito takes pride in doing it himself. No sort of work is too mundane for Armandito: filling a pail of water from the faucet at the back of the house; retrieving a page of instructions for a power tool that's blown away in the wind; looking for a trowel or pair of clippers that's been left behind. Just being with his father was a treat; translating for him was pure joy; and proving himself to be good at this work seems something he's waited for all his life.

Just as apparent was that, for Armandito, I am the boss, a wealthy white man whose life is a mystery to him, a mystery about which he is curious but respectful. He rarely asks me questions about anything other than the work we're doing. I'm an even greater mystery to Armando who, I imagine, grew up in poverty in Mexico and has not had the schooling Armandito has had here in this country.

During summer months, we pulled thistles and installed irrigation. In the fall we laid two-hundred-and-fifty feet of PVC piping a foot-and-a-half deep to replace the leaking pipeline from the pump up to the house. To construct wooden planter boxes, we bought lumber, metal grating, electric screwdriver, and screws. Neither Armandito nor I have ever used an electric screwdriver. I read the instructions aloud and Armandito translates. Armando uses the electric screwdriver for some time before letting his son have a go at it. Finally, I'm given a chance to try it. There is no rush, we have all the time in the world. When Armandito talks to his father, he calls him "Poppy" (the sound of the Spanish *Pape*), which makes me smile every time I hear him say it.

The three of us work every Sunday regardless of the weather. On a Sunday morning, during the second summer we were working together, I say to Armando and Armandito that I know Mexico is going to play in the final rounds of the World Cup in about an hour. Armandito translates for his father and Armando says something. Armandito is silent. I ask Armandito what his father said. Armandito doesn't answer and looks back at his father who is using a shovel to break the large basalt rock at the bottom of the pit he's digging to plant a persimmon tree. While Armando is getting a long iron bar from the garage to break the rock, Armandito tells me the Mexican team is on television now, but his father said they've agreed to work with me on Sundays and they'll stick by their word.

When Armando returns, I tell him that it's okay with me if he and Armandito go home to watch the soccer match. He looks at me squarely in the eye as he says, "We work." I say it would be a shame if they missed the game. He mumbles something to Armandito before walking up the hill to his van. He drives to the verge next to where we're working and parks it. After fumbling around for the Spanish language station, he turns up the volume so he and Armandito can listen while we work.

When the announcer's voice is loud and excited, and when the crowd is cheering, I ask Armandito what's happening. He tells me not only about that play but also about the stars of the Mexican team, the team's surprising rise from a second-tier status, their best player's injury mid-season and his return for the finals, the team's style of bringing the ball up-field rapidly with delicate passes which often bring unfair off-side calls from the refs who don't understand the way the ball is moving. When the Mexican team loses after tie-breaking penalty shots, tears well in Armandito's eyes as his father quietly says something to him. I later ask Armandito what his father said. He tells me he said it's only a game, and it doesn't matter. Armandito tells me he replied, "It matters to me."

It's unclear to me if Armando is documented, but I assume he is because he and his family drive south every Christmas to spend some time with Armandito's aunts, uncles, and cousins in Los Angeles. They then drive further south to visit family and friends in the small town near Guadalajara where Armandito's parents grew up. Armandito told me his mother, Maria, is very religious and goes to church every day before taking a bus to the hotel where she works as a chambermaid. The church in the town where she and Armando grew up and where they were married has a statue of the Virgin Mary that wept when his mother was a few months old. Each Christmas she has requests for the Virgin Mary. I met Maria one morning when she dropped Armandito and his father off. I said hello to her. She replied only, "No English."

———

I don't know if I could have done something to end the battle — perhaps sacrifice is a better word — in which Arthur and Walter were locked. I'm responsible for Arthur now.

After graduating from community college, Arthur cut himself off entirely from our parents. He drifted for a number of years. He lived modestly. When I visited him, I brought groceries. He wouldn't accept money from me.

Each time he and I spoke by phone, I felt relieved that he hadn't killed himself or gone to live under a bridge. He told me that the man who lived in the apartment next to him played music all night to try to get him to move out of the building. Arthur dressed in food-stained clothing; his complexion was sallow; dishes were piled up in the kitchen sink. He preferred talking with me by phone to my visiting. He would ramble from one thought to the next without a connection that I could understand.

Now and again, Arthur comes to spend some time with me in the country. These stays are difficult for him because he values solitude above all else. But solitude can devolve into a playground for his voices. I think our father's voice tells him he's worthless, not worthy of the space he occupies in this world. But maybe the voices are the only things he has that tell him that he exists at all.

When living with me, Arthur spends most of his time in his room but is finely attuned to every occurrence in the house. He knows how many times I get up at night and the precise words used in the commercials of the music station on the radio I listen to. I don't know how he does this, but he can tell me how much gas I have in my car by listening to the sound of the car as I drive up the driveway.

Though living with me at the house can be less intense for him than life in his apartment in the city, it's never easy. He eats very little and never likes the food I prepare, even though it's what he's asked me to cook. In the evenings, he goes to his room immediately after deciding he's had enough to eat, leaving the cleaning up to me. He doesn't tell me when he plans to return to his apartment. I arrive home after work and find that his things are gone, he's taken a cab to the bus station. He doesn't leave a note, just dirty dishes in his room.

Perhaps what most interests Arthur when he stays with me are the Sunday mornings I spend with Armando and Armandito. He listens to every shade of feeling in our exchanges when we're close enough for him to be able to hear what we're saying. He continues watching us long after we've moved to a place where he can no longer hear what we're saying.

One Sunday, when I finished work with Armando and Armandito, and I returned inside, Arthur was puttering around the house, picking up a book, then a framed photo, and then a section of a newspaper, pretending to look at each item before returning it to its place. "Never seen anything like it," he says, apparently to himself. He putters some more. "The father's proud of the boy. Worries terribly about him."

"Worries about what?"

"He worries the boy is too soft-hearted for the world, worries the boy'll be eaten alive."

"Arthur, why won't you let me introduce you to them?"

"I wouldn't want to change anything about them. I can do that to people."

———

One Sunday morning, Armandito, now 16, a large, heavy-set boy, taller than his father, with peach fuzz on his upper lip, finds a moment when we are out of earshot of his father. He tells me he's seen from his window at home two men who look like gangsters approaching from the back of their apartment building. He ran to warn his father about the men he'd seen. There's nothing that these men could want from his father, Armandito tells me, because his father doesn't have anything except the van, which isn't worth much. Armandito says he watched as his father walked down the concrete steps at the rear of the apartment building. He and the men stood about ten feet apart. The exchange of words took a few minutes. Armandito could hear them speaking but couldn't make out the words. Afterward, Armando said nothing about what had happened.

Armandito tells me he's worried that the men are from the INS and that his parents will be deported. He says that he, his younger brother, and his sisters are legal residents because they were born in the U.S. I tell Armandito I think the men are unlikely to be INS agents because both his parents must be documented since they have the papers to drive into Mexico and return to the U. S. every Christmas. Also, it seems to me that INS agents don't meet people they're targeting in the back of their building after dark.

A severe recession caused work to dry up for the concrete company where Armando worked. Armandito tells me the company has laid off the Hispanic workers and kept the white workers to do the little work the company still has. Armando continues to come to the house on Sundays, but he's lost weight and moves more slowly. I take him aside one Sunday and tell him I can lend him whatever he needs until he resumes work. He shakes his head and says, "*Gracias* ... no." Armandito tells me his father finds as much work as he can at the Boyes Hot Springs pick-up site where I used to hire men.

The two men Armandito saw behind their apartment building return every couple of weeks to talk with Armando in the dark. Armandito tells me this with fear in his voice I'd not heard before. Just before he and his father leave one Sunday, he tells me that he's now playing tackle for his high school football team which holds practices on Saturday and Sunday mornings, so he won't be coming to work unless they don't have a practice on a particular Sunday morning. His brother, Noah, younger than Armandito by four years, will be taking his place.

On his first Sunday, Noah slips out of the passenger door of the van and trails his father rather than standing next to him as Armandito had on his first morning. When we shake hands, his hand feels firm in mine. Noah is a handsome boy. He speaks English without a hint of a Spanish accent. I later learn that Noah does very well in school.

Noah shows no interest in helping with what his father and I are doing. He is quietly disdainful, volunteering nothing. When I ask him to do something, it takes him five minutes to begin to do it. As time goes on, his stubbornness becomes increasingly provocative. One day after the football season is over and Armandito is again coming to work each Sunday, I take Noah aside and ask him, "Why do you come here with your father and brother? You clearly have no interest in being here."

"My father makes me come."

"Why does he want you to come here?"

"He wants us to learn how hard it is to earn a living."

Armandito and Noah seem to have learned different lessons from coming to work with me. Armandito has learned that if you want to make money and earn a living, you must learn your trade and do it well. Noah has learned that earning money from manual labor is not for him; he's going to make a living in some other way.

The four of us occasionally drive to businesses selling fencing materials, gravel, slate, and the like. There is space in Armando's van for only two people once we pick up bulky material, so we take my car as well as the van. On one of these mornings, Armandito jumped into the passenger seat of the van, leaving Noah no choice but to ride with me. During the drive, I ask Noah what he's studying in school.

"English, math, biology, social studies, and I don't know ... something else."

"Is there anything that interests you?"

"Not really. It's not hard. I don't have to study very much," he says.

"Is there anything you'd like to learn about?"

"Rap music."

"What about it?" I ask.

"How to write it, how to play it, how you sing it, how to record it, and how to distribute it."

"Do you write any rap music?"

"Some. I'm in a band," he says.

"What's the name of your band?"

"The Barons."

"Your last name."

"Yeah."

"What do you want to do when you grow up?"

"Compose music, maybe perform it, but definitely write it," Noah replies.

"I don't know much about rap music."

"You wouldn't."

"Is there any chance I could learn?"

"Not much," he says. "It's not something white people can really hear or dance to, but they act like they can. But they look pathetic."

"Do you write the lyrics to the songs?"

"Yeah."

"Can you tell me any of them?"

"No, they have to be sung to music. You probably like the Beatles."

"I do."

"You have no idea how old and tired they are. You maybe heard of Beyonce and Eminem and Tupac."

"Yeah, I have."

"I figured," he says. "But you never heard of real rappers — Louis Cole, Black Midi, Dr. Dre, Lil Wayne, and ASAP Rocky."

"No, I've never heard of them."

"Didn't think so," he says.

"Do you play your music for Armandito?"

"Nah, he's not interested."

"Have you ever tried?" I ask.

"I know him."

Noah, grudgingly, continued to come to the house with his father when Armandito was unable to come. One day, when Noah and I are standing alone in the shade under a stand of redwoods, he mutters, as if talking to himself, "I have a question for you."

"Are you talking to me?"

"You think you can give me an honest answer to a question?" Noah asks.

"I won't know till you ask the question."

"Have you ever been with a Mexican who wasn't working for you?"

"No, I guess I haven't," I say.

"Why not?"

"Because there aren't Mexican men who've been colleagues at work. That's mainly how I meet people."

"So, you don't go to a health club."

"I do."

"And there are no Mexican members of the health club you go to?" he asks.

"I've never asked myself that question."

"Maybe there aren't Mexican members because it's too expensive or they don't need artificial ways to get exercise," Noah says disdainfully.

"Noah, you've got something you want to say to me, so why don't you just go ahead and say it?"

"No, it's not a single idea I have in mind, it's more that I imagine you think you know my family because you work with my father, my brother, and me. But you don't know the first thing about us. You don't know what we eat, what each of us says at the table, how many of us sleep in each of the bedrooms and in each of the beds, whether we have relatives living with us. I guess what I want you to know is that you don't know me at all."

"Do I get a chance to say anything?" He looks surprised that I have anything I want to say.

"Whatever."

"Everybody has a public side and a private side. The members of our families know a lot about our private side. Nobody else knows us in that way. But other people can get to know us, can't they?"

"Yeah, so what?"

"The fact that I pay you and your father and your brother to help me garden doesn't prevent me from getting to know your public side and a little of your private side," I say, doubting Noah believes a word of it.

"Whatever ... You have a wife?"

"My wife died ten years ago."

"You have kids?"

"Two boys, now grown."

"Where are they?"

"They live on the East Coast. I go out and see them a few times a year and they come out here."

"Why are they living out there?" he asks as if trying to wrap his mind around this kind of family.

"They went to college out there, got jobs there, got married there, they just stayed."

Noah doesn't say anything for a while.

I ask, "You have more questions?"

"Nah."

———

Noah, though a coerced and unhappy participant, reconciles himself to serving as a translator for his father. I have to get used to the idea that Armandito won't be coming on Sunday mornings. I sorely miss him. I received more than I gave, the privilege of witnessing love being given and received, ordinary, unselfconscious love, a form of love I had rarely experienced with my own father, a love I feel for my children. I hope that they feel loved by me in the way Armandito feels loved by his father.

Armando worked six days a week for the concrete company and a half-day for me. I knew that this was a punishing schedule. I told myself that this was what he wanted for himself and for Armandito. It's easy to see the sadness on Armando's face now that Armandito is no longer working with us. He no longer tries to speak and understand English. Without Armandito, he has lost the pleasure he once took in doing the work. I think that Armando can't understand Noah, a boy who is unable to appreciate what his father has been through as he tried to make enough money to support his family in a country where he didn't know the language and was looked down on for being poor and Mexican. Noah seems to view his father as a man of a bygone era, a man who is hopelessly lost.

Not long after they return from Christmas in Mexico, Noah tells me that now that football season is over, Armadito will be coming to work again, and Noah won't be coming any longer. The following Sunday, as he steps out of his father's van, with his large chest and protruding belly, Armandito looks as if he's been inflated like a balloon. He now has a deeper voice and a round face on which a big crop of whiskers is growing. But he's still the boy I've come to love with his bright eyes and warm smile that still have some of the child left in them.

He grins widely as he sees me and pulls me to his large chest. He tells me that he's going to graduate from high school in a few months. I ask him what he's going to do when he graduates. He says he plans to go to the local branch of the state college. "I want to take courses in police work so I can do the stuff like the people do in CSI programs on television."

He invited me to his high school graduation. "It's no big deal, but I thought I'd invite you even if you can't make it."

When I arrive on the day of the graduation, it's an outdoor ceremony at which Armando's family has gathered around a row of folding chairs toward the rear. There are a few hundred people attending. Armando greets me warmly. Armandito's mother looks at me with a gaze that says she is at a loss to understand why I've come to the graduation. Armando, with a gesture of his right arm and hand, shows me the chair they've saved for me. I stand by myself because no one but Noah speaks English. After Armandito has received his diploma, I leave after thanking Armando and his wife for inviting me to the ceremony.

The following Sunday, when Armandito comes to work with his father, I give him a laptop computer as a graduation present. I tell him that he'll need this when taking his college courses. He's thrilled and promises me he won't use it to play video games.

One Sunday morning during the summer I ask Armandito about the courses he'll be taking when college begins in the fall. He tells me that he hasn't figured out how to register online and was told he'll have to come to the campus in late August to register in person. But at the end of the summer, he tells me he'd gone to the campus to register but was told that all the courses that interested him are full.

Again, Armandito stops coming to the house to work, this time because he's selling kitchen knives door-to-door. One Saturday, he comes by and shows me the knives he's selling. He tells me he has a sales pitch he uses when trying to make a sale. I ask him if he'd like some practice delivering it to me. After we've put in some work on his sales pitch, I buy one of the knives. It seems to me that his career as a knife salesman will end when he tries selling his wares to someone who isn't a friend or relative.

———

In the fall, Noah resumes working with his father. Early one Sunday morning, before he and his father are to come to the house, Noah calls me saying his father's van isn't working so they won't be able to work with me that day. It's uncertain how long it will take to repair it. After some weeks of receiving this same message from Noah, there comes a call that is different. He tells me his father isn't feeling well so they won't be coming. I don't ask in what way his father is ill for fear of putting pressure on Armando to work on the only day he has off. These calls from Noah continue for a few more weeks before he tells me his father has been admitted to the hospital. They don't know what's wrong.

The following Sunday I call Noah asking how his father is. He tells me that his father is in the ICU because he has a virus. I want to talk with Armandito who I know will give me a fuller picture of what's going on, but he's not living at home, and I don't have his phone number. I don't even know if he owns a cell phone.

A few Sundays later, I tell Noah I'd like to speak to Armandito. Noah says he'll tell him to call me. Later that day, I receive a call from Armandito who tells me his father was very weak for a month before he was hospitalized. He had resisted the ER doctor's recommendation that he be admitted to the hospital for tests and treatment.

Armandito tells me, "My father is afraid of doctors and hospitals. He couldn't get out of bed at home. A week and a half ago, me and Noah carried him to the van and I drove him to the hospital. They put him in the ICU where they don't let visitors in because they bring in germs and things that can make him and the other patients even sicker. My mother and me and my brother can see him now because he's in a different ICU, one for the lungs. He's very sick, a lot skinnier, he's got tubes in his nose and arms, and he's connected to beeping machines. Is that normal?"

"Yes, it's normal for a patient in the ICU to have tubes to feed him, equipment that keeps track of how his heart is doing, and a mask over his nose to give him oxygen to help him breathe."

When Noah next calls, he asks, "Would you go see my father in the hospital?"

"Why do you think that will help?"

"You're white and not Mexican. I don't think they're doing everything they can for him."

"Noah, do you have any reason to think that?"

"Not really, I know everybody's supposed to get equal treatment, but that's not the way it works."

"Well, we're not going to change that in the next few days."

"After that, he'll be dead anyway. So don't trouble yourself."

"Is my visiting him all right with your mother?"

"She'll say no."

"Why would she do that?"

"She doesn't trust anybody, especially white people."

Armandito, grabbing the phone, says, "You'll go see him?"

"If your mother says it's okay. Tell me how he is now."

"Not so good. He's very tired. I don't see the point of you going to visit. He'll hardly know you're there, and he won't want you seeing him the way he is."

I don't go to see Armando because Maria refuses to even consider it.

After a month, Armando is transferred out of the ICU into a regular hospital room. Then, in November, after three months of hospitalization, Armando is released. I call each week to see how he's doing. Armandito now has his own cell phone, so I can talk with him directly. He tells me his father isn't able to walk more than about twenty yards before collapsing.

As they do each year, Armando and his family make their pilgrimage to Los Angeles and then to the town in Mexico where Armando and Maria grew up, and where their families continue to live. Armando insists on making this trip despite his weakened condition. In January, I receive a call from Armandito telling me his father has died.

——

I was not invited to Armando's memorial mass in LA. I would have liked to have gone but knew I'd have been a distraction for Armando's wife. She feels I pushed Armando to his breaking point by making him feel obligated to work on the only day of the week he could rest. I wonder myself whether it was good for Armando to work on Sundays, but I felt that he wanted to come to the house on Sundays because he enjoyed working with me and his sons.

After Armando died, I noticed that small things — a four-inch flashlight, a pair of gardening gloves, a Phillips screwdriver — weren't where I expected them to be. I attributed this to my own increasingly unreliable memory. I expected I'd come across the things that I'd misplaced, but I never did. I don't lock the side door to the garage. There was nothing of any value there, aside from the personal value the tools held for me.

It was sometimes months between the small thefts, which created the illusion that each theft was the last. There was little doubt in my mind that Noah was the thief. I had stolen his father from him, and he would not let me forget it. It was out of the question either to call him and accuse him of being a thief or to notify the police about absurdly insignificant thefts carried out through a door I never lock.

It took me six months to cease hoping Noah would get tired of reminding me of the harm he felt I'd done his father. I decided to write a note to him which I taped to the side door of the garage.

> *Dear Noah,*
> *I miss your father very much. I wish I had seen that the work he was doing for me was too much for him. I think that the best thing for you is to be a man your father would be proud of.*
> *Raymond*

A week or so later, the letter was taken from the door and the thefts ceased.

——

When Walter developed Parkinson's, our house became a medical clinic. Mom took over the job not of a nurse but of a doctor. Not long before he died, she asked me to come home for a week to help her take care of him. While I was there, on getting up from his chair in the living room, he fell and was unconscious for a short while. Mom told me to call 911 and tell them we need an ambulance to take him to the ER.

I made the call. Walter yelled at me, "Raymond, cancel it. Do you hear me, cancel it."

"Don't you dare cancel that call," Mom yelled back.

Walter looked at me pleadingly. He was a grown man who had the right to decide if he wanted an ambulance. But Mom had decided that he did not have that right.

The ambulance arrived in a few minutes. I opened the door to five or six paramedics and ambulance drivers who were about my age, perhaps a little younger. He sat patiently as they took his blood pressure, measured his oxygen level, and took an EKG.

He then said softly but firmly, "I count six of you here and I thank you for making this visit, but I'm not going anywhere so I'd be grateful if you'd leave." They made a case for taking him to the ER. He steadfastly said no. They had him sign a release saying he had refused to be taken by ambulance to the hospital. I could hear the front door close behind them as they left. Mom removed herself to some corner of the house.

Walter said, "Look, Raymond, I'm sorry I put you through this. It has nothing to do with you and yet we've dragged you into it."

"Why didn't you want to go with them?" I said.

"Because there's nothing they can do for me. Parkinson's eats you up little by little until there's nothing left. It's eating your mother up, too. You have a life of your own to attend to."

"My life," I said. "I'm a widower with two sons living on the East Coast."

"Don't give in to self-pity."

"How can you live with what you did to Arthur?" I asked.

"I can't live with it."

"So, you have a way of erasing it."

"No, a way of carrying it," Walter said.

"What are you talking about?"

"I'm the same person that I was, but a little older and wiser."

"Don't you see what you're doing?" I said. "You have an answer for everything. It's as if you can write your life as you write the lives of the political figures in your books. You can't rewrite what happened as you'd like it to have happened. You don't understand that."

"You don't believe people can change," he said.

"I believe it can be done, but I don't believe you've done it," I said.

"You can't feel that I'm any different from the person you remember me to be?"

I couldn't betray Arthur by agreeing with Walter, though there was some truth in what he was saying. By this time, I was no longer so certain that Walter had "caused" Arthur's mental illness, though I was sure he could have been a better father to Arthur and me.

———

Three or four years after Armando died, while sitting at an outdoor table at a restaurant in town, I recognize Armandito with a small group of people being shown to a table not far from mine. The woman walking beside Armandito is pushing a baby carriage. I make my way over to say hello.

Armandito greets me with the smile of a small child thrilled to see his father back home after work. He introduces me to his wife, Evelyn, who is not Hispanic. He tells me that Evelyn teaches nursery school. Their eight-month-old daughter, Louisa, is looking up from her carriage to see what the commotion is about. Armandito gathers her up and in one motion puts her in my arms. All of a sudden, I'm holding his little girl firmly to my chest. Along with Armandito and his family is a handsome man with long black hair. It takes me a moment to recognize Noah. He seems glad to see me, which surprises me.

Armandito tells me, with evident pride, that he works at Angelo's Deli, a well-known luncheon place at the edge of town that began as a beef-jerky stand. After talking briefly with Noah and Armandito, I realize we are blocking the path of the waitresses. I tell Armandito I won't disrupt the family outing, I'll visit him at Angelo's.

On a Saturday afternoon at a time when the deli isn't busy, I walk through the door to find Armandito behind a refrigerated display case in which there is an assortment of deli meats, pastas, lettuce, tomatoes, onions, and three sorts of potato salad. There is no one in the deli besides Armandito and three middle-aged women with whom he works. Armandito greets me with a firm hug. My hands reach around only the edges of his large back. The women, seeing I am a fatherly friend of Armandito, welcome me and tell me how dear a person Armandito is and how much they enjoy him. They know him as Armando.

It is a warm spring afternoon. Armandito and I talk outside near the edge of the parking lot behind Angelo's. He tells me about the trip south their family took the Christmas when his father died. "We always stop to see my aunts, uncles, and cousins in LA for a few days on our way to Mexico. When we were there, my father spoke to me in private because there was something he wanted to tell me. He'd never asked to talk with me in that way. He said he wanted me to know that if I meet a girl and we like each other, it's all right to do what feels right. I think he wanted me to know this because my mother is so religious. The trip that year was something that my mother wanted to do very badly because of the statue of the Virgin Mary in the church there. She wanted to ask the Virgin Mary to cure my father. Very soon after we got to the town, my father had a heart attack. The doctor in the town told him and my mother they couldn't treat him there, so he'd have an ambulance take him to Guadalajara. My father said, 'No, I want to die here.' He died the next day. They buried him in the church cemetery next to his parents."

I tell Armandito, "He loved you. I could see that in the way he was with you, right from when the two of you started working with me when you were 10 years old. He looked at you with such love and pride."

"Yes, I knew that even then."

"And it was just as clear how much you loved and admired him, and he knew that."

Armandito takes out his cell phone and shows me photographs of his wife and daughter. He tells me that he and his family are living one floor down in the same apartment building where his mother lives. Noah lives with her in her apartment.

"What's Noah up to?"

"He's a music composer. He writes lots of different kinds of music. He's trying to sell his music to performers. He says he's getting close to selling some. I help my Mom and him a little. I don't mind really."

I tell him that Noah had told me a long time ago that he wanted to write rap music and perform it and sell it.

I ask, "Did you ever find out who those men were who talking with your father behind the apartment building?"

"He never told me. He was scared of them. My guess is that they wanted him to bring drugs back from Mexico in his van. A van filled with a man and a woman and four children might not get stopped and searched. I don't know. And I don't know how he got rid of them. I think maybe they gave up on him, saw that he wouldn't do what they wanted, no matter how they threatened him, but that's just a story I made up. Or maybe he couldn't take it and got sick from the pressure of it."

———

Now, many years since Walter died and Arthur died, I'm an old man. Armandito continues to work at Angelo's where he's become manager after the older women retired. Noah continues to live with his mother. I visit Armandito now and again to reminisce about the days when he and his father and I pulled weeds, hooked up drip systems, learned to use an electric screwdriver, and listened to the Mexican team playing for the World Cup. We speak, putting aside the sadness of it all.

— CALL IT FRIENDSHIP —

A list of hand-written names accompanied by phone numbers and skill level was pinned to a knackered bulletin board next to the door of the squash court. From this list, squash players looking for a partner chose the name of a person to call for a game. Neither Eric nor Martin could remember which of them had made the initial phone call. The Jewish Community Center housing the squash court was, at the time, a rather run-down place. Martin was 30, Eric 43, when they arranged a time to meet for a game. Eric was a silver-haired Englishman, Martin a curly-haired American who had recently moved to the city. No personal information — in fact, almost no information at all — was exchanged in that initial phone call other than the hours each of them was available to play. Martin wasn't interested in feverish clashes that determine who is the better man. Nor was he looking for a friend. He was looking for someone to play squash with. He wanted a gentleman's game and he wanted to be able to rely on the squash partner, a partner who would not cancel games minutes before the arranged hour.

On the day they first met in the lobby of the JCC, Martin and Eric shook hands, exchanged greetings, and walked downstairs silently to the locker room where a gay man with pink hair checked their membership cards and confirmed that they'd reserved the court. They found empty lockers a yard apart. The thought occurred to Martin as he was getting into his squash clothes that it isn't often that you take off all your clothes minutes after you've met someone.

As they walked toward the court, there was awkward silence. The stairs they climbed were dimly lit by light bulbs in metal cages. They stooped as they walked through the door into the court. The four walls had the feel of the face of an elderly person on which, over the years, lines had been drawn by black streaks left by hard-hit balls.

They became regular squash partners and soon worked out times when they could play four or five days a week. One might think that this would soon become confining for two men with jobs, but they rarely missed a game, even on Christmas Day, a holiday not celebrated at the JCC. They each approached the game playfully: what ordinarily mattered did not matter. Their conversations didn't involve disclosures concerning childhood experiences, current family members, or occupation. In fact, they rarely spoke about anything but the weather and local sports teams.

There seemed to be an unspoken agreement not to ask any personal questions of one another, not even where they lived, jobs they held, whether they were married or had children. It was only after years of playing squash together that Eric volunteered that he worked as a salesman of products for dental offices ranging from magazine subscriptions, to bibs for patients, to finely crafted surgical instruments. Whether Eric was satisfied with his work was not something he cared to reveal.

Martin's occupation as a copyeditor by day and a novelist by night seemed to be a pair of activities with which Eric had no familiarity or interest. Eric's heart resided in soccer — or football, as he called it. He had been a professional soccer player for Liverpool United. He spoke not at all about experiences he'd had playing soccer and spoke only briefly about the ankle injury that ended his career, and the name of the opposing player who had tripped him. Martin knew little about professional soccer but was impressed by the fact that Eric had played for Liverpool United. For Martin, Eric's career as a professional athlete accounted for the fact that Eric was his equal at squash, though thirteen years his senior. Martin, over time, had come to see Eric as an amiable squash partner, but not a person with whom he would become friends. Though Eric was never late and rarely canceled a game, Martin imagined that he could disappear, and Martin would not have the slightest idea where to look for him.

There were experiences with Eric that compounded Martin's uncertainty about who he was to Eric. On Christmas Day of the third or fourth year they played together, Eric brought a box of cheaply packaged chocolates. Martin suspected that the chocolates had been given to Eric at a company Christmas party or by one of the dentists with whom he did business, and Eric was now passing them on to him.

One day, Martin, perhaps in an effort to interject something that he thought would be of interest to Eric, volunteered that George, the older of his two sons, was playing high school soccer. The following day Eric brought a few copies of *The British Football Weekly* for Martin's son and then regularly asked about how George was enjoying soccer and the papers.

Martin lied telling Eric that his son took great pleasure in reading *The Weekly*. After about a year, Eric stopped bringing the paper.

——

Martin and Eric settled into a pattern of playing squash together four times a week which lasted more than twenty-five years. After six or seven years, they gradually became more open about occurrences in their lives, how long they'd been married, that they had children and grandchildren, where they lived before moving to the city, and a little about their childhoods. But very few words were spoken about regrets and disappointments they lived with, grief they'd suffered, or unrealized hopes they had.

After more than a decade of playing squash with Eric, when Martin called Eric's home to cancel a game, Eric's wife, Flora, answered the phone. Eric was not at home. She told him, as a confidence, not a scolding, "He really gets quite upset when this occurs, far beyond what I would expect of a man who rarely shows his feelings. Your game means a lot to him." Martin wasn't surprised that Eric was upset when Martin canceled a game; he was surprised Eric knew he was upset by it.

Eric was sparing in any mention of members of his childhood family and spoke least of all about his father. When he did mention him, he did so in hushed tones as if his father, a very private man, would suffer if the information were made public. Eric told him that his father managed a chain of bakeries in Liverpool that were owned by the Broadhursts, a wealthy Liverpool family. During the war, the business struggled. The company could not afford to continue paying the salaries of all the employees when sales had sharply declined due to the poverty that was overtaking the city. Eric's father proposed to the Broadhursts a plan in which all the employees would accept pay cuts, so no one would lose their job. He had included in the pay cuts a cut in his own salary and a reduction of the payments made to the Broadhurst family. The family rejected the plan. Eric's father was told to tell the staff that there would be layoffs. When he told the employees about the impending layoffs, he felt he had betrayed them, which tore him apart and may have contributed to his early death at 58, when Eric was 19.

Eric liked telling stories about Churchill, a man who was both a hero and an alcoholic, though Eric spoke only with admiration about the fact that Churchill drank a bottle of scotch the morning before his meeting with Stalin and Roosevelt. Perhaps his favorite story, which he told many times, was about how Churchill, at 91 and close to death, was overheard telling a Black Molly in his beloved tropical fish tank: "Darling, I do love you ... I would make love to you if only I knew how." Not knowing why, Martin was saddened by Eric's stories about Churchill. This sadness grew, particularly during the last years they played squash together.

———

Martin received a call from Flora one day when he and Eric were to play squash. Through tears, she said that Eric had had a bad fall on the tiles next to the pool at the JCC that morning. After being taken by ambulance to the emergency room, he was admitted to Saint Michael's Hospital. She was with him, now, in his hospital room where he was comatose and unresponsive.

Martin visited his room at Saint Michael's that evening. When Martin opened the door to Eric's hospital room, he found Flora along with Eric's son and daughter from his first marriage standing at the near side of Eric's bed. Introductions were made before Flora and the adult children stepped back so Martin could stand next to the bed on his own. Eric was comatose, attached to blinking monitors, but not to any breathing apparatus. On taking his hand, Martin was surprised by its warmth. He did not speak out loud to Eric, he spoke silently to him. As he was talking, it occurred to him to tell Eric something that he had not said before — even to himself — that Eric was not only his squash partner, but his closest friend. A friend with whom he'd delighted in behaving like a small boy as they changed the time on the clock outside the squash court so they could begin their game a few minutes early, or held up an imaginary trophy showing it to the crowds in the stands on all four sides of the court, as if at Wimbledon.

———

Two days later, Eric died.

Martin asked Frank, the man who managed the locker rooms, to post a notice saying that there was going to be a memorial service for Eric in a week's time at the Swedenborgian Church at Lyon and Clay Street. Frank, a Sister of Perpetual Indulgence, tipped his hat to Martin in a way that conveyed not his own pain of loss, but his recognition of Martin's pain.

At the entrance to the Swedenborgian Church on the evening of the service, Martin watched Russell, a man he knew from the JCC, being lowered to street level in his wheelchair from the back of a transport van. It was about six-thirty on a brisk early autumn evening. The pale light of the moon cast a bluish film over the people standing about. Russell and Martin shook hands. Russell's grip was enervated. They'd never met anywhere other than at the JCC or the outdoor space between the parking lot and the front door of the building.

Russell was in his late 30s, a black man with a square face, penetrating eyes, and light brown skin. He said he'd been an innocent victim of a gang war during which he was hit in the temple by a stray bullet, which left him paraplegic. It also left him with severe migraine headaches that lasted for a week at a time and then would lift and leave him in a daze for another few days. He had a broad smile, but the desolation in his eyes was complete. Russell and Martin would talk for a few minutes as Martin walked from the public parking garage to the entrance of the JCC. Russell knew the day and the hour of each of the games Martin and Eric played. Before each game, Russell would meet Martin outside to exchange a few words, even in the rain and cold.

The JCC was located next to a ten-story housing project in one of the most dangerous parts of the city. Membership at the athletic facilities of the JCC was available to the occupants of the project at a greatly reduced rate. Martin joined this JCC despite the neighborhood because it was close to the advertising agency where he worked. He liked this JCC in part because its members, at least the ones who used the locker room, were not professionals or upwardly mobile businessmen. They were predominantly middle-class and working-class men, a fair number of whom were from the housing project.

When Martin and Russell first met, they would talk about sports and happenings at the JCC. Early on, Martin stopped and talked with Russell out of pity, and only later, as he came to know Russell, did he grow to genuinely like him and admire him for his sense of humor that edged out bitterness. He was a kind man and an intelligent man who had been deprived of a decent education. He told Martin about his life as a long-haul truck driver. The animation in his voice, the graceful movement of his hands, and the smile on his face at these moments reflected the pride he took in having been able to support himself, his mother, and his two younger brothers when working as a trucker.

"Now that I can't drive, I've got nothing to show anyone. When I left trucking, I lost that feeling of having the world by the short hairs. You know what I'm saying? The money was good but that wasn't the most important thing. What I lost is the good feeling about myself, a feeling that I'm good at something."

As time went on, Russell spoke openly with Martin about what he called his "hall of shame," his sexual impotence. He was still able to flirt with women who came by, he said, but he felt like a fraud, like he was acting, like he was playing music on a player piano. "You've seen the way women pass me by without looking at me, like I'm not there, like I'm a homeless man on the street. Be honest, you've seen them doing that."

"I'm ten years older than you, Russell, but I might as well be sixty years older for all they look at me."

"You're married, so you shouldn't be looking for being looked at. You got anything you're ashamed of, Martin?" A startling question, a very personal question. He hesitated before saying that he did, but he didn't like thinking about it, much less talking about it. Russell was quiet as Martin stood next to his wheelchair under the battleship-gray sky, surrounded by the sound of boys joshing one another as they walked into the projects.

"I trust you, Russell, so I will tell you in confidence what I've never said to anyone, not even my wife, though she knows about it because she was there." Russell was silent with his head turned to the side and upward to look Martin in the eye. "When my mother was dying at her home here in the city, this was five or six years ago, I was crazed about making money at work and completing a novel I was working on. I knew my mother liked seeing me, her firstborn son who she was very proud of. Yet, I didn't visit her very often — hardly at all really. She died alone. Even the caregiver who was looking after her was out of the room when she died. I can never forgive myself for that. Even my wife doesn't know the whole story."

Russell was silent but kept his eyes fixed on Martin's. "You made a bad mistake, and you can't forget it 'cause you never stop learning from it."

"Shame never leaves you alone. Some people might be able to put it behind them. I don't know what that means."

"You're nursin' it."

The two were silent for a minute or so and then Martin left without bidding Russell good-bye.

———

Martin could never guess what he and Russell would talk about each day as they made their way from the parking lot to the entrance to the JCC. Once Russell said to him, "What you got on your mind there, Mr. S." He called Martin "Mr. S" as an abbreviation for Mr. Squash Player. Martin didn't like Russell's calling him Mister because he felt it alluded to the class difference, the race difference, the money difference, and the health difference between the two of them, though these were undeniable facts.

"You've got an eye for reading my innards," Martin said.

"What's going on with you?"

"I'm worried about my younger boy, he's four, he's not doing well. He can't sleep through the night, he wakes up with nightmares every night, I don't know what to do."

"If you don't know, nobody does."

"I tried bringing him to a child psychiatrist, an old lady with a good reputation, and she just told my wife and me that we shouldn't have had children if we weren't prepared to sit in a chair in his room and stay there all night, every night till he can sleep through the night."

"Man, that's wicked."

"You've gone through much worse."

"Don't give me that. This wheelchair isn't a badge of honor, it's got me, so I've got no choice in the matter."

"Well, that's courage."

"No, it ain't."

The two then paused and looked toward the street where cars and buses were backed up.

One day Russell came toward Martin hurriedly, closer to the parking garage than usual, straining to get his wheelchair to move as fast as he could wheel it. "You got to help me about something."

"Slow down, Russell."

"They got medicine now. My neurologist told me 'bout it, a new drug for migraines they got out now, only the past couple months. It might work for me, but each pill costs $90, and the State Disability people say that it's not covered. You think you could write a letter for me to the Disability people to ask them to pay for the medication, at least part of it?"

"I'll help you write the letter."

"Come on, that ain't right. You're a writer. That's what you do."

"You're a smart man, Russell. I'll help you write it."

"You serious? You gonna play games with me 'bout this?" His eyes brimmed with tears as he locked his eyes on Martin's.

"It's not a game. We'll get this done quickly."

Russell spun his wheelchair around in circles.

"I'm not going to bullshit you about this. You show me a sentence or more each day I'm here and it'll get done fast," Martin said.

"You gotta get me started. I can't write. Couldn't in school. Not even close."

"Just tell me what you want to say."

"I want them to pay for the medicine."

"Alright, write that down. That's a good sentence. Try to think up another one. It's no harder than talking and you're a good talker."

"Don't fuck with me. That sentence isn't worth shit."

"When I get finished here today, you show me what you have, and I'll help you make it better."

Russell swung his chair around and wheeled toward the entrance of the JCC.

As Martin was leaving the JCC that day, Russell ushered him to a bench outside. Because of the glare of the sun reflected off the torn white sheet of paper, he had difficulty reading. "'To the state disability insurance. I got real bad migraine headaches and need the new medicine they call Imitrex, but they cost $90 a pill. Can the insurance pay for it?' I got no more after that."

"Anybody help you write that?"

"No, there's nobody I know that can write."

"Do you know how well you write?"

"I know I'm not stupid. A bullet in my head tore up muscle-control parts of my brain, not the mental part."

When the letter was finished, Martin typed it and mailed it to the State Disability agent that Russell dealt with. There was no response. Russell's neurologist told him that his campaign was "admirable but hopeless."

———

As Russell wheeled his chair off the lip of the transport van the evening of the memorial service, Martin said "hello," but Russell, preoccupied, didn't reply. He muttered something about the jostling of the van. He wasn't ready to go in, he said, as if Martin had urged him to do so. People were only beginning to arrive at the church. Russell used his powerful upper arms to wheel himself up the gradual incline at the front of the church to the end of the block where the sidewalk leveled off. Martin followed. Very quietly Russell said to Martin, "I'm sorry to ask you this, but could you look at the urine bag aside me." With his right hand, Russell lifted the thick, black plastic flap behind which there was a translucent collection bag filled with dark yellow urine.

Kneeling on the sidewalk in the dim light, Martin could see that a tube had become disconnected and was spilling a thin stream of urine over the side of the bag down onto the rubber wheel of the wheelchair. He told Russell what he saw. Without a word, Russell reached into a side pocket out of which he pulled a packet of alcohol wipes. "It's asking a lot, I know, but would you connect the tubes and clean up the mess." Martin reconnected the tube, and as best he could, wiped up the urine that had spilled.

When Martin finished, Russell said, "Give me the wipes, they're a stinking mess. I'll get rid of them." He stuffed them into a pocket of the wheelchair on the side opposite Martin. He handed Martin fresh alcohol wipes. "Use these on your hands."

Martin hadn't seen Russell since Eric died two weeks earlier. Trying to make conversation, Martin said, "Eric's wife called me to tell me that he'd had a fall and was taken by ambulance from the JCC to the ER at Saint Michael's. She hadn't been able to talk with him because he was in a coma."

"Eric himself called me," Russel said. "He was in the ER up at Saint Michael's. He called me and said he was waiting on a gurney in a hallway. He said he was tired, and his head hurt where he fell."

"Eric's wife told me that he fell after he'd been in the pool trying to learn how to swim," Martin said.

"I thought it was only black people that don't know how to swim." A sly grin lit up Russell's face, which had the soft, creased look of a well-worn catcher's mitt. Russell went on: "He told me that, during World War II, his family, in Liverpool, England, five of them, said good-bye each night 'cause they didn't know if they be alive to see each other the next morning. That's a real kick in the head for a kid?"

Eric had told this story to Martin, too. Because Eric said so little that was personal, he'd thought, when Eric told him about this, that he was telling Martin something that he would entrust only to him.

"He hired one of the swimming instructors there to show him how," Russell said. "He didn't want to die before setting right what his big brother done to him."

Eric had told Martin the story about his older brother throwing him into the water from the bridge over the Mersey in Liverpool to teach him how to swim. This story, too, Martin had taken as a personal gift from Eric that was meant only for him.

"What else did he say when he called you from the hospital?" Martin asked.

"He said the people at the JCC called an ambulance that brought him to the hospital. He still had his bathing suit on. He said he was shivering on the gurney in the hallway. He was just filling the time by calling me while he waited."

"You were the last person he talked with before he died."

"I s'pose."

"You kept him company while he waited — not just waiting for a doctor but waiting to die."

"He took me in his car to some places over the bridge, the cliffs right after you get over the bridge." This, too, surprised Martin.

"How'd he get you and your wheelchair into his car?"

"He has one of them big cars, a Lincoln I think."

"How'd he get you into the car?"

"He lifted me into the passenger seat. I helped him with my hand on the roof. He folded the wheelchair, stuck it in the trunk. His wife's family owns motels, one's up north near Arnoldsville. We drove up there once, a couple-hour drive. We didn't get out the car. Eric got us some burgers and fries at a diner-like place. We ate in the car in the parking lot. He said he'd done some tours up there for people staying at the motels his wife's family had."

"You and Eric were good friends."

"I guess, but not like my trucker friends. We talked by phone while we was driving. Even if one of us was in Idaho and the other in Virginia, we talked together. When I stopped at a truck stop off the highway, and there was a trucker, we were friends, no matter who he was or what color his skin."

As Russell talked, Martin found himself searching for something he felt Eric had entrusted only to him. He recalled Eric's having once asked him, when they were about to leave the squash court, if he had any sedatives he could give him. This request was the most personal thing Eric had ever said to him. He'd told Eric he had some at home and would bring them the following day. Eric added, "It's a tenant in a place I own who won't pay the rent and won't get out." Martin brought some tablets the next day. Eric said he was grateful. No mention of the incident was ever made again, but Martin experienced Eric's request and his explanation, if only a single sentence, as an act of great personal intimacy.

———

Martin walked next to Russell down the steep sidewalk to the front of the church to say hello to Ito, another friend from the JCC, who was standing at the edge of an illuminated circle cast by the lights at the church entrance. Ito was, as always, at ease in his formality. He was a Japanese man who could have been anywhere from his mid-50s to his mid-60s. He was a quiet, dignified man with high cheekbones and angular facial features, a short man, five-foot-three or five-four.

At the JCC, Ito had been, at first, a fleeting presence that was gone before Martin could turn his head to see who or what was there. Gradually, over a period of years, this diminutive Japanese man slowed his pace as he passed by. When Martin was walking out of the JCC one day, Ito appeared in front of him as naturally and unobtrusively as a leaf falling from a tree. He said, "I'm pleased to meet you. My name is Ito." He bowed from the waist and with two hands outstretched offered Martin his card on which his name was printed in a delicate cursive font, along with a phone number on its lower right corner. On handing Martin his card, Ito stepped back and again bowed. Martin introduced himself and then bowed to Ito.

This exchange felt to Martin to be an event of consequence. Martin later understood this event to be Ito's communication of his commitment to honesty and respectfulness in a relationship that was then beginning.

At the church, Ito, as always, was dressed in a black suit, white shirt, and dark tie. Martin sometimes imagined that Ito worked in an expensive men's haberdashery or perhaps as a personal assistant to a wealthy man. He never learned how Ito supported himself. His suit was old, a bit shiny at the lapels, but never stained.

Once they began to stop and talk at the JCC, Ito told Martin he was born and raised in Tokyo. Martin had spent a year teaching English at a boys' secondary school in Tokyo. By coincidence, the tiny apartment Martin had rented looked out onto a large public square in the Ebesu District, in which there was a cemetery where Ito's parents were buried.

As they stood outside the church, Ito described his father's funeral. Ito was only eight at the time. His father was one of the directors of a large Japanese insurance company. "After he died, my father was laid in his own bed at home for a night before he was taken to the funeral home where a group of about fifteen friends and family, including me, watched a Buddhist priest and his novitiate cleanse his body, dress him in a dark blue kimono and then lift the body and place it in the coffin. I was allowed to put a piece of candy into the coffin to reflect my father's and my own shared love of sweets." Ito spoke in a soft voice and used very simple words and hand movements to describe people and scenes.

Martin imagined that Ito had never married and lived alone. He further imagined that Ito was gay and had been a disappointment to his parents for not bringing them grandchildren and for not creating the appearance of a conventional life.

Ito was a gentle man who Martin had come to know a bit through their talks about life in Japan, the Japanese language, and contemporary Japanese authors and artists whose work had been translated into English or exhibited in America. Martin felt when talking with Ito as if he were holding an injured bird in his hands, a bird that, with time, batted its wings less violently, and eventually quieted peacefully.

"The moonlight is beautiful tonight," Ito said. "The street falls down this hill like a river into the night."

"It's you who's creating that river," Martin replied.

"I thought, at first, Eric was a vacant man hidden behind his English accent and decorum," Ito commented. "After a time, I thought he might not be empty, but indiscriminate: anything was to be tolerated so long as it asked nothing of him. And finally, I found him to be discriminating. He discriminated between people he found trustworthy and those he didn't."

Martin replied, "Eric was thirteen years older than I am, but he always seemed to me to be my age. I do that with people — whether they're 10 years old or 90 years old, I speak with people as if they're my age."

"Years are calendar time," Ito said. "People don't live calendar time, they live time that twists and bends, goes forward and backward."

Martin was never sure to whom he was talking when he was with Ito. Ito created a particular presence, a solemn presence, a presence marked by acceptance of everything as it is, while always remaining a step removed.

———

Martin and Ito, who had walked down the hill a bit to talk alone, slowly returned to the murmuring crowd outside the church door. Ito and Russell said hello to one another in a way that seemed cordial, but somewhat cold. This didn't surprise Martin. Even though both men spent some of each day at the JCC, their interior lives were so vastly different that it was difficult for Martin to imagine they even noticed one another when their paths crossed.

Ito and Martin then took positions on opposite sides of Russell's wheelchair looking out over the street that shimmered under the moonlight. After a time, Martin recognized the silhouette of a man across the street, a man from the JCC who never divulged his name. As Martin crossed the street to say hello, the man retreated. He was a man in his 30s who, like Ito, wore clothes that seemed to hide rather than express who he was, except for his shoes. So far as Martin knew, this man wore the same clothes every day: black pants washed so often they were wearing through, a gray T-shirt or sweatshirt bearing no lettering or emblem. He painted his hi-top sneakers various colors, often pale oranges and greens, seemingly repainting them every two or three weeks. Not only were his sneakers painted in pale colors, but the man himself seemed to be painted in similar hues: he had blonde hair with a touch of ginger, facial features that seemed soft and pliable, a body that was neither muscular nor flabby, neither tall nor short, in brief, he was an eminently forgettable man, except for his painted hi-tops, which made him unforgettable to Martin.

For years, when Martin came upon this man at the JCC, he would nod but received no indication that the man noticed him. It didn't seem to Martin that he was being snubbed; it seemed that he was nothing to this man. Eventually, for no reason Martin could grasp, the man slowed his pace as he passed by. This slowing grew into an exchange of nods, then an exchange of hellos, and eventually an exchange of a few words.

One day, this man with his painted hi-tops, without saying a word, and with a diverted gaze, placed in Martin's hand an 8" by 12" piece of orange paper. At the top of the page was the logo and address of a local theater. Below the logo was printed the name of a play to be performed, the name of the playwright, times and dates of performances, and a list of the names of the actors and director. Martin asked if he was one of the actors listed here. The man nodded with a faint smile crossing his face. Martin asked which of the names on the flyer was his. The man took back the announcement from Martin and ran his forefinger down the list of names as if looking for his own name, and then as if he'd been unable to find it he returned the piece of paper to Martin. Martin thanked him for letting him know about this play. Before Martin finished speaking, the man was walking briskly down the hallway.

Feeling that this man had entrusted an aspect of himself to him, Martin attended a Sunday matinee performance of the play. The theater was small, with about twenty rows of seats. While people were making their way to their seats, the curtain was already open revealing a canvas backdrop on which were painted floor-to-ceiling shelves crammed with books. Martin had the feeling he was in that room, a room that was at once familiar and mysterious. As the play was being performed Martin recognized the man with no name who was playing the role of a character who, despite the fact that he was a minor character, was pivotal to the action of the play.

After the play, the actors disappeared backstage where Martin presumed they met with friends. The information about the play that Martin received at the performance listed the actors in alphabetical order as the announcement had done. That felt right to Martin. The man with no name had invited him to a performance of a play, not to a ceremony disclosing his name.

Martin had come to feel that the five of them — Eric, Russell, Ito, the man with no name, and himself — were living a form of theater together. As in legitimate theater, the play as it is being performed feels more real than the people who are performing and more real than the people in the audience.

———

When an usher at the Swedenborgian Church announced that the service was about to begin, Martin wheeled Russell to the small elevator in the anteroom of the church and met him upstairs at the level of the sanctuary. With Russell beside him, they made their way through the cold and sparsely furnished reception room. The sanctuary itself was smaller and warmer than Martin had expected. There was a fireplace at the front of the room, tall vertical windows on the left, and a wooden domed ceiling. There were about thirty rows of long benches covered by tan seat cushions on either side of a central aisle. The room was devoid of crucifixes, stained glass, icons, sculptures, or any other suggestions of a particular religion.

Russell positioned his wheelchair in the aisle at the left end of an unoccupied row of benches. Martin took the seat at the end of the bench closest to him. They were soon joined by Ito and the man with no name. Though tonight they were gathered as a group, Martin understood that the four of them were not a group. Each of the other three had a relationship with him that felt so delicate that it could not be sustained in the presence of anything in the world outside of itself. This was true of his relationship with Eric as well.

A pastor, dressed in a dark suit and tie, stepped up to the dais. He began the service by thanking Eric's friends and family for gathering there. There were about fifty people present. Toward the end of the service, Martin was startled when the pastor asked him if he would say a few words because Flora had mentioned him as Eric's closest friend. Martin had not planned to say anything but now felt obliged to come up with something. He stood and awkwardly made his way past the knees of Ito and the man with no name and then around Russell's wheelchair. It was difficult to find his footing; his legs seemed to be failing him. Once at the podium, he apologized for not having prepared something to say. He said that Eric and he had played squash four days a week for more than twenty-five years. "You get to know someone well that way. During that time, our public veneer wore off, and in its place, evolved forms of childishness and solemnity and frivolity and trust and fierce loyalty.

"I am here with three friends who knew Eric for many years. Russell Green was a man Eric liked and admired for the strength he shows every hour of every day in not allowing the sorrows of his life to defeat him. He was the last person Eric spoke with before he lapsed into a coma a couple of days before he died. Eric also admired Ito, another friend, for the quiet dignity with which he carries himself, dignity that connects him as well as separates him from the people he cares about. And the friend who is a stage actor was, for Eric, a man he liked for the humor expressed in the way he paints his high-tops, an expressiveness that reminded Eric of Charlie Chaplin. He was grateful to each of these three men for making his life fuller, each in his own way." Martin felt he was not lying, but the word "friend" did not seem quite right to describe what each of these men was to Eric.

Martin made his way back to his seat where the three men were staring forward, studiously avoiding eye contact with him. As Martin sat there, he wondered if he had betrayed them by speaking about them publicly when they were not public people. Their tie to Eric had not been in the form of words spoken; it lay, he thought, in the wordless theater they each performed with him. Eric and the other three lived in a world configured by what you see in the eyes of another person; by simple acts such as taking a wheelchair-bound man for a drive; by the respect and affection conveyed by faint bows given and received; and by the sound of spoken words.

At the end of the service, Russell wheeled his chair into a corner so as not to obstruct the slow line of people making their way to the exit. Martin said good-bye to Flora and to Eric's son and daughter. As he turned to leave, Flora lightly squeezed his elbow, turned slightly toward him, and said under her breath, "Don't worry, I know." She quickly turned away after saying these words, not giving Martin the opportunity to say or ask anything. He then walked through the anteroom, down the stairs, and out of the church doors to the street.

On the sidewalk, the three men gathered next to Martin, each unsure whether his connection with Martin would continue in the absence of Eric and the squash games.

Martin shook hands with Ito and the man with no name who then wandered separately into the night. Martin told Russell he'd stay until the van arrived. As they waited, Martin said that Flora had said something to him that puzzled him. "She said she knew, so I shouldn't worry about her." He asked Russell if he knew what that was about. Russell nodded, his eyes fixed on a nearby bench.

Still not looking at Martin, Russell said, "I'm not good with saying things, but there's something that I think you might want to know, but you might not."

"Know about what?"

"About Eric?"

Martin became flushed as if one of his own secrets were going to be revealed.

"I don't know if you want to know some things, I can't know that."

"It must be something serious, something important that I don't know."

"No, it's not so important."

"So, tell me what it is I don't know."

"It's about Eric. He had his secrets. He was a good man, but he had his secrets. We all do. I don't want to be spreading gossip."

"Russell, what are you trying to tell me?"

"The four of us knew Eric for a long time, you knew him twenty-five years, right? I don't know where it started, but Ito saw Eric in one of those big fancy department stores downtown, and Ito was with a friend from England, and he introduced his friend to Eric. Afterwards, Ito's friend said Eric isn't from Liverpool, his accent is from a place in the middle of England, near Birmingham, I think is what he said. He even knew the county his accent was from. He said it was a lower-class accent covered by a more middle-class accent. After that, Ito and I suspected something's not right with Eric's story. We liked him a hell of a lot, but we were curious too, maybe we shouldn't of been. I liked Eric, more than any white man I know ... other than you," he said with his sly grin.

"But what?"

"It's just that Eric had his secrets. His story wasn't like he told it to you. I don't want to tell you more if you don't think you want to know more. I can respect that."

"Russell, please get to what I don't know."

"A lot of Eric's stories about himself he made up. He wasn't a soccer player for Liverpool and his family wasn't in Liverpool during the bombing of Liverpool like he says. And the story he liked to tell about his brother throwing him off the bridge into that river in Liverpool...."

"The Mersey."

"Yeah, maybe it was a river somewhere else, but not that one in Liverpool."

"He just made up those stories?"

"That's what I'm thinking."

Martin countered, "We all make up stories about ourselves, stories we sometimes get ourselves to believe, but they're just stories. Isn't that right?"

"Yeah, I s'pose. Maybe I've said enough, too much."

"I'm not shocked, so far. Nobody's been hurt by these stories, have they? One man thinks his accent isn't a Liverpool accent. That's it."

"No, I couldn't find Eric on the Liverpool team the years he's saying he was. This isn't a big deal. There's nothing wrong with making things up if you're a good person aside from that, and he was."

"And the story about being thrown off the bridge into the water by his brother, is that a story too?"

"Maybe it's true in another city. I don't know, but not in Liverpool." Russell fell silent, his eyes focused on something indeterminate behind Martin.

Martin asked, "And the story of his father taking responsibility for firing some of the staff of the company he managed during the war. You know that story?"

"Yeah, he told it to me, but it's like something you see in the movies. It could be true. I don't know."

Martin was stunned by what Russell was telling him. The "evidence" Russell was giving was flimsy.

"Russell, do you hear yourself talking in this way about a friend?"

"He's a friend but these are facts."

"The 'facts' aren't facts, they're guesses, they're ideas."

"Come on, man, don't do this to me."

"Do what?"

"Paint me as a traitor. I don't mind the stories. That's who he was. I like him and feel sad for him."

"You're inventing the man you feel sad for," Martin said.

"I'm sorry I said things to you about Eric. I should a kept them to myself."

———

Though he didn't maintain his membership at the JCC, Martin came by, now and again, to say hello to the three men. During one of these visits, Russell said, "This JCC is about to close for a couple of years while they demolish it and build a new one." For Martin, these words were like an announcement of the closing of a long-running play.

— Sophie's Story —

Why do they say you can kill two birds with one rock?" Paul asks nobody in particular at the breakfast table.

"What are you talking about, Paul?" his mother says.

"I just wanted to know why people say it."

His father, Robert, looks on as if he were about to step forward to separate two boxers locked in an illegal hold.

"Don't you see? Paul's turning an old saying into something original," his sister Sophie, volunteers, bouncing her right foot up and down under the table, looking at her mother out of the corner of her eye.

Their mother, Marjorie, exhales a short, almost inaudible, snort.

"I didn't mean anything by it," Paul says.

"Sure, you did." His mother turns as if to get up but stops herself.

"It just was going through my head, so I asked, but I didn't mean anything by it."

Turning to Paul, Sophie says, "Killing two birds with one stone means you can sometimes get two things done at the same time if you plan it well. You used the word rock instead of stone, which is much better. It's a kick. A rock sounds much bigger than a stone and it's funny to think of someone throwing something that big at birds, and killing two at the same time, don't you think?"

"I guess."

Marjorie, now lost in her own thoughts, surveys the kitchen, which she sees as run down — linoleum curling, paint flaking, appliances forty years old — but feel she's too old and too tired to do anything about it, even to buy a new stove. She also feels too tired to change anything about herself. She's been through too much already.

Sophie studies her mother's face, as she often does. Her mother's disdain is writ large across her face, like the bold black lettering on a marquee of an abandoned movie theater. The reasons for her mother's bitterness are as well-hidden as they are innumerable. *As well-hidden as they are innumerable* and *writ large like the bold black lettering on a marquee of an abandoned movie theater are quite good*, she thinks. The meaning isn't all that clear, but it doesn't have to be clear. Is Shakespeare clear? In fact, good writing shouldn't be clear.

Life isn't clear. Life told in words is much more interesting than life itself, she likes the sound of that, too.

Their mother, by pulling her chair back from the table, gives the signal that breakfast is over. Robert stands and proceeds to methodically collect the forks and spoons, the dishes, then the cups, saucers, and bowls, and finally the juice glasses, carrying them all to the sink in as few trips as possible — a satisfying challenge he sets for himself at the end of breakfast and supper, Sophie reckons. In one continuous motion, he turns on the faucet, opens the dishwasher door, rinses dish after dish, and utensil after utensil. He then passes each piece from his left hand to his right, and then, to its designated place in the machine. He does this as if doing a crossword puzzle far too easy for him, but which nonetheless passes the time in a not unsatisfying way. After drying his hands with a dishtowel, folding it, and placing it to the left of the sink, he turns to face the breakfast table, pleased to see that it is exactly as it was when he first stepped into the kitchen an hour ago, leaving no evidence that anyone has been in the room, except for Sophie who, he just now realizes, has been watching him all the while. Her father nods to her trying to act as if he knew she was there all along.

Robert then walks through the dining room with its reproduction Queen Anne table and matching chairs and chest of drawers. He inherited these from his mother. They look completely out of place in this 50s-style ranch house. On entering the bedroom, Robert walks to his cedar dresser at the opposite end of the room. It puzzles him, as it does each morning, why he has a mirror on top of his dresser when the mirror only hurts him with its response to his gaze. To the left of the dresser stands a sliding-door closet where a row of suits and a tie-rack dangling striped and paisley ties await him. Marjorie, across the room, is dusting the silver-framed photographs on her dresser.

"I can't just … I don't know," she says with her eyes brimming.

"I don't know either. I just try to live with it."

"That's so you, Robert. It's not me."

"Please, Marjorie."

"I don't know what to do. I suppose there's nothing to do."

"What could we have done?"

"I should have begged that doctor. If I had gone to see him and begged him to do something. I knew something was terribly wrong. I kept telling him, 'He's got the face of an old man.' I knew that wasn't right. Any other mother would have done something. Why didn't I? I keep asking myself why I didn't."

"Please try not to do that to yourself. It doesn't do you any good. You did all anyone could. You see that, don't you?"

"I don't, really."

Robert, standing quietly across the room from Marjorie, now looking at her from a distance that seems vast, trying to picture a different life, a family with children all of whom are alive. Try as he could, he couldn't imagine it.

———

Sophie and Paul are halfway to school, so deeply immersed in their own thoughts that they mechanically cross streets without paying attention to traffic. They are an odd-looking pair. Sophie is 14, Paul is four years younger. Sophie, a freckle-faced girl of pale complexion, is a bit short for her age, she thinks. Paul is a gangly boy who seems never to have proper footing. He remembers saying to Sophie, "Just think of it — it's a wondrous thing, the distance around a circle divided by the distance of a straight line across its center. That's *pi*." Which brings to his mind, "at sixes and sevens" — numbers that still sting. He heard his mother saying that about him. He pictures the numbers, sixes with their heads sticking out above their round bodies, and sevens, like soldiers standing at attention, but leaning back, dressed up with that belt across their waists, a flourish that his mother adds, but no one else does.

Sophie worries about her father as she walks. How long could he put up with her mother's continuous reign of disapproval? "Reign of disapproval," a good phrase. Rain and reign. Her mother's reign. She is imperious, another word Sophie likes. They won't get divorced like her friend Annie's parents did. It's just that her father seems defeated; no, not defeated, servile to her mother, a good word, "servile," that's what he is, he does what she tells him to do, though Sophie doesn't like to think of him that way. He isn't pathetic in the eyes of other people — the eyes or is it I's of other people? He's adorable, even if her mother doesn't think so. Handsome in his own way — he looks a little like Paul Newman, and a little like Dustin Hoffman. He's strong, but he doesn't pick fights and never yells when he's angry. He isn't afraid to stand up to bullies. At the supermarket, a man was yelling at a small boy in a stroller. He went up to the man and said, "Please don't frighten the boy that way." The man was embarrassed, tried to ignore her father; other shoppers stopped and stared at the man.

Her mother isn't a bully, she's a sniper. She sneers and snorts and snoots, if that's a word, it alliterates with the other two, she's that way, not just with their father, with everyone, but least of all with me, why would that be? Other girls talk about the scalding fights they have with their mothers, but I can't imagine fighting with her. She wouldn't stoop to screaming or yelling. Sophie had seen her cry only once when the gardener cut the ivy off the front of the house. He said the ivy digs holes in the wood, but her mother cried, only that once. Girls at school cry a lot, mostly when with other girls in the girls' lavatory. Sophie wonders what it would feel like to cry in the girls' lavatory. Neither she nor her mother cry. Maybe we're less feminine than other girls and women. We both hate shopping for clothes, listening to saleswomen lie about how good you look in a dress or a blouse and pushing you to buy the more expensive thing which "is to die for" — to die for, how can they allow those words to pass between their overly lipsticked lips?

Sophie and Paul, on coming within range of the animal-like shrieks of children playing in the schoolyard, part pensively.

———

Their father had been behaving strangely at dinner, Sophie thought. He was quiet, then blurted out some inane question that he posed to her or Paul about what she and Paul did at school and after school, till Sophie couldn't stand it any longer, and asked him who he met at the water cooler at the office that day, and how many cars were in the parking lot when he arrived that morning, and how many telephone calls he'd received today. She knew she'd overdone it and felt bad about it — "bad," a terrible word. Is the right word "ashamed" or "guilty" or "penitent" or "regretful?" In any case, he hadn't deserved to be humiliated. No, humiliated isn't the right word. He's comfortable with himself, so you can't humiliate him. If you try, it's you who feels ashamed, not him. That's what's most maddening about him — he opens himself to reprisal because he says what he thinks, which gets people mad. After supper, she hears him pacing in the kitchen, which is directly below her bedroom. She isn't surprised to hear him climb the stairs with heavy feet on each of the stairs. He knocks softly, at first almost imperceptibly.

"Sweetie, may I come in?"

"What do you want?"

"Just to talk."

"About what?"

"Stop it. Can I come in?"

"If you must — and it's 'may I,' not 'can I.'"

He opens the door as she slides off her bed into her desk chair in one motion. It feels like a game of musical chairs that her father has lost, leaving him standing awkwardly in front of her. Obviously, he couldn't sit on her bed.

"I'd like to talk to you, but not here. Let's go to the study."

"Where 'family talks,' or should I say 'sermons,' or maybe 'inquisitions' take place?"

"Give me a break, Sophie. You're much quicker on the draw than I am. How many times do you have to shoot me before you're certain I'm dead?"

"A bit histrionic, don't you think, Dad?"

"All right, are you finished with the massacre so we can go and talk?"

She follows him down the stairs. The study is a small room with one double-hung window which at this hour stares back at you, reflecting your own image. Sophie has to admit it is a tranquil, if nondescript, room just a few steps down the hall from the kitchen. The room might have been a pantry when the house was built in the 1930s. It is a small room, with a faint kitchen odor, not knowing how to stuff into itself the two armchairs, heavy oak desk, and an uncomfortable straight-back wooden chair. Built into the wall to the left of the desk are floor-to-ceiling bookshelves that house, most prominently, The *Britannica Encyclopedia*, ten or fifteen years out of date.

Her father takes a seat in one of the two armchairs, and Sophie squirms in the other as if it were a piece of clothing much too big for her. He is uncomfortably close. He leans forward as if about to put his hand on her knee, but she knows he would never do that. Sophie sits straight up in her chair.

He says in his most compassionate, sonorous tones, "Sweetie, I worry about you sometimes."

Sophie suspects she knows what is on her father's mind but is afraid that she could be wrong and it is something much worse — sexual, a subject she definitely does not want to talk about with him. It seems to her that he knows next to nothing about the female of the species, though to be fair, he seems to see them as a mystery he'll never understand, not as inferior, or having a misconfigured — Miss Configured — body.

"I love the things you've written that you've shown me," he says.

"But what?"

"But the amount of time and energy you put into it…."

"Where is this coming from? Has she sent you to deliver her disapproval of me as a … as a what … a grandiose, self-important child? If you've got something to say, say it and be done with it. And if you've got nothing more to say, admit that and be done with me."

Her father smiles broadly as Sophie speaks, seeming to find her cute, which infuriates her.

"To tell you the truth I really don't know how to help you and I won't even try, but please talk to me about one thing."

"You're making my imagination run wild. One thing you want your fourteen-year-old daughter to talk to you about. What could that be, I wonder?"

"Calm down. I just want to talk to you about your writing."

"So, what do you want to know — my favorite American poets?"

"Now you're just making fun of me. Couldn't we just talk for a minute? That's all I'm asking."

"What do you want — say it straight out."

"I worry that you love writing too much."

"Too much for what?"

"Too much for anything else to grow. Too much for you to grow."

"You think I should have a boyfriend and posters of movie stars and rock groups on my walls, and teddy bears lined up across my pillow, and a music box with a ballet dancer on top that twirls to the tinkling of 'Blue Danube.' Just say it if that's who you want me to be." She can feel her face redden as she speaks.

"No, that's not what I'm thinking."

"What are you thinking?"

"People mature in junior high and high school."

"I'm not 'people,' in case you haven't noticed." She's glad she isn't a girl who cries.

"Let's both calm down and see if we can start again. I'm not trying to tell you that you should be anyone other than who you are. You're more than I could ever imagine my daughter, any daughter, could be. I hope you know that. You know I've felt that way from the day you were born, don't you?"

"Don't sweet-talk me," she says unconvincingly.

"You love writing and you're a very fine writer."

"Thank you, but what?"

"But there's a difference between liking to write and using it... ."

"Finally, it's on the table. Using it to avoid real life. That's it, isn't it?"

"Yes, I guess it is."

"You guess? You were thinking it before you even knocked on my door, weren't you?"

"I was, in a way, but I didn't know how this was going to go."

In a slow, measured voice, which surprises her, she says, "If you listen carefully to yourself, you're telling me that I'm not a real writer, I'm a teenager who uses writing to avoid life."

"I wouldn't put it that way."

"So what do I have to do to prove to you I am a writer and not a self-deceiving 'teen' — isn't that the disgusting word they use to refer to people my age? The word carries a stench that knocks me over every time I hear it. Teens are very excitable, they think they know everything, they do dangerous things without giving it a second thought, they show poor judgment, they drink and smoke and get pregnant, that's what they're like, aren't they?" She can now feel her cheeks glowing a disgusting shade of scarlet.

"Sophie, Sophie, Sophie, I don't know how to say it, but you already know it — how much I love you and how enormously proud I am of you. You're one of a kind — not a kind for everyone — but just right from where I'm standing." His eyes brim with tears.

"Daddy, don't just say that... ."

"I don't lie. You know that about me. I've never in my life said anything I mean more than what I just said."

"You know you can get sloppy sentimental, don't you? It's embarrassing sometimes," she said.

"No, I wouldn't have described myself that way."

"Daddy, let's talk about something else."

"About what?"

"About how you act sometimes."

"What are you talking about?" he replies.

"You can act like you're not there sometimes as if you don't see what's going on."

"What are you talking about?" he repeats.

"I'm talking about the way you let Mom say mean things to Paul like she did this morning."

"The answer to your question is simple. If I told your mother how to talk or behave with you and Paul, she'd feel terribly hurt. You have no idea how hurt she'd feel. And it wouldn't make her change the way she behaves."

"So, your job is to protect her, no matter what effect she's having on anyone else?"

"That's one of my jobs, yes," he says.

"Do you have any other jobs?"

"Sophie, that's enough."

"It's not enough for me. Don't you see, you have to ask more of yourself," she says.

"If I knew how to do more I would."

"Don't act pathetic. That's not an excuse."

"I wish I could tell you the whole story, but I can't," he says.

"Why can't you?"

"Because it's between Mom and me."

———

As the school year proceeded, it was apparent that Sophie was withdrawing from the world. She went directly to her room on returning home from school. She was quiet at the dinner table. She often said she wasn't feeling well and couldn't go to school. When forced to go, she left school during the middle of the day.

At 14 this is to be expected, Marjorie and Robert repeat to one another until it becomes a chant devoid of meaning. Sophie, in her room, is fully occupied by her thoughts and by the words her thoughts come wrapped in. She has arrived at a fundamental truth about her life: life is lived as subject matter for writing, and the richest part of life isn't life with other people, it's life with one's imagination, which is limitless. All that she will ever need as a writer is what she already has within her. Reading is frustrating because as she reads, she either finds herself editing the bad writing or standing in awe of the good writing, doubting she can ever write the way her favorite writers do. Whether she is reading bad writing or good writing, she becomes impatient to write something of her own.

The school was at first understanding about her parents' difficulty in getting Sophie to attend school, but after a couple of months, they became impatient.

In response to her father's knock on her door after dinner, she yells defiantly, "Go away."

Through the locked door, he says quietly but audibly, "I wish I loved you less because then I'd be free to leave you to do whatever you want to do."

Silence.

"I can't stop loving you so I'm going to do everything I can to help you with whatever's going on." He is silent for a little while and then asks again if she'll allow him to come in. Sophie, embarrassed by the thought that Paul and her mother are listening to her father's pleading, grudgingly opens the door.

Her father takes a seat at Sophie's desk chair while she, in her flannel pajamas, sits on the edge of the bed closest to him, her bare feet on the floor.

"Sophie, I understand that you don't want to go to school, but I don't understand why. You're very bright and a talented writer."

"I'm not a talented writer. Hemingway and Steinbeck are talented writers. I'm just a schoolgirl trying to learn how to write."

"Yes, I know that you feel that way, but I'm entitled to my opinion if I don't force it on anyone else, aren't I?"

"Please don't try to manipulate me with compliments about my writing, so I'll reciprocate by going to school. Isn't that what you're up to?"

"Sweetheart, I'm not trying to win you over or get you to go to school. I want to find out what you're feeling and see if I can help you with it."

"Why do we have to begin with the premise that I've got a problem and you have the answer? Maybe you're the one with the problem and that problem is me."

"I don't want to debate with you. You're right that I have a problem and the school has a problem. The school is telling me that by state law you must go to school until you're 16."

"And if I don't, what happens? They'll get very, very mad."

"Sophie, I'm not interested in their story, I'm interested in yours. Would you please tell me why you don't want to go to school?"

Sophie lifts her head from the spot on the floor where her eyes have been fixed and glares at her father.

He tries to gather himself, removing his glasses and rubbing his eyes. "The school is hounding me about the fact that they have a responsibility to provide you with an education...."

"Stop it. Try to think for a minute. I've decided I won't be attending school. I don't have a problem with that. You don't have a problem with that. It's their problem. Let them be the big bad wolf and try to blow the house down."

"I don't know what to say. I have it in my head that children go to school until they finish high school and then decide if they want to go to college or go to work."

"Did someone tell you that this is what children have to do in order to grow up?"

"The law defines the meaning of the word child. You're a child until you're 16. That's the law. I didn't make that up."

"I don't care who wrote it." The fury in her voice stuns Robert.

"You're very bright...."

"Yes, I know, so just say what you want to say."

"The school tells me that when a child has shown a protracted period of absenteeism...."

"Is that a word? Maybe you mean truancy."

"... they are obligated to get testing to determine how to help the child with the problem they're having."

"I'm the problem?"

"Yes, you're their problem."

———

It surprised Robert that she acceded to testing. He imagined that Sophie agreed to it because she thought that the person administering the tests might be an interesting person with whom to spar. Maybe it was something else, he didn't know.

The psychologist, Dr. Nevin, is a cool, self-possessed woman in her 50s who, Sophie thinks, has almost no feminine features other than the annoying high pitch of her voice. As the testing proceeds, Sophie becomes tired of reading ink blots, making up stories for characters on 3" by 5" cards, remembering series of numbers forward and backward, and doing jigsaw puzzles.

Prior to the meeting with Dr. Nevin to get the results of the testing, her mother said to Sophie that she'd come to the meeting with the psychologist if Sophie wanted her there, but she wasn't in the mood to listen to someone who pretends to be able to see into other people's minds. Sophie felt the same way but wished her mother would attend anyway.

After what seemed to Sophie to be an endless chain of clichés about how each girl has a unique mind of her own, Dr. Nevin finally got down to the business of reading the tea leaves.

"The testing shows that you are a very intelligent young lady, Sophie. Your creative quotient is significantly above normal as is your intelligence quotient. You are in the very gifted range. There is something, however, that drew my attention, which may be something you've noticed about yourself. It involves missing the contextual cues. Let me give you an example. Do you remember on one of the cards I showed you the scene in which a man is holding a child? You thought the man was the child's father, but you didn't seem to notice that the man was holding something behind his back that could have been a knife or a gun and that the room and the man's face were drawn in ominous dark ink. Do you remember that?"

"Kinda. Well, yeah, I remember. It seemed sorta ordinary."

"You had trouble with reading comprehension. After reading three of the eight passages, you said that you didn't understand what was happening. You remember that?"

"Yeah."

"It's hard for you when there are multiple characters."

"Yes, guilty as charged."

"You know that we're not here to find you guilty or innocent. We're here to find out if there are problems in learning and then try to help you with them."

"Should I become somebody else?"

"No, of course not. When you were asked to group silk, paper, and canvas, you grouped canvas and paper."

"Yes, you can write on canvas and paper, not on silk."

"You still would group them that way?"

"Maybe you're supposed to group silk and canvas because they're both fabrics, but I can't see that that's the right way to do it."

"I think your way of doing this sort of thing is original, your own, but it makes it hard to see things the way other people see them."

"So, what am I supposed to do to be like everybody else?"

"Sophie, stop it," her father interjects. "You know what Dr. Nevin means."

"Stop what?" Sophie barks. "I'm just trying to get her to tell me who I'm supposed to be." With her voice quavering, she says, "It's my brain she's dissecting."

"I'm trying to talk with you about patterns of thinking that may make it hard for you to understand what you're reading or hearing."

"I don't have any trouble reading or hearing. I read all the time."

"Sophie, let me put it this way, you have trouble seeing what is obvious to other people, which makes it harder to understand what is going on in a classroom."

"You're saying I don't see what you see. So is it you or is it me that has the problem?

"Sophie, try to calm down." Her father is leaning out of his chair in Sophie's direction.

"Are the people in the trains to the concentration camps causing a problem because there are so many of them that they make it very hard for the trains to run on time?" Sophie doesn't expect either of them to understand what she's asking.

"Sophie, what are you talking about?" her father asks.

Sophie groans. "Is it the people in the trains to the camps that are the problem?"

"I don't follow you."

"Don't you see that it is the wholesale murder that's the problem, not the people being transported? Maybe it's not me who's the one who doesn't see the obvious?"

Dr. Nevin presses her point: "I'm saying that your way of organizing what you see is confusing because you have so many storylines going that you get confused about which one is the predominant organizing one."

"Check-mate."

"That's enough, Sophie," her father says, his voice now fatigued.

"How much can I expect to receive in disability payments for my impairment?" Tears well in her eyes.

"Sophie, please try to bear with me," Dr. Nevin says.

"What if I enjoy making things up more than I enjoy seeing them the way I'm supposed to see them?"

Dr. Nevin, now says solemnly, "Sophie, I'm here to tell you what I see in the testing, not to dictate the right way to do things."

During the ride home, Sophie and her father are quiet. Her father breaks the silence saying, "I just wanted to have you listen to her to see if there's anything at all that's useful."

"Don't feed me more BS."

"The tests showed how your creative thinking gets in the way of other kinds of thinking."

"She said I can't see what's obvious to everyone else. What am I supposed to do with that?"

"You're not supposed to do anything with it."

"Why do you say that?" Sophie says with a note of hope in her voice that surprises her.

"Because you're just fine as you are. I'm not trying to change you into anyone else."

"What is the school going to do with the test results?"

"They may find a way of making school more interesting for you."

"Or they may put me into special ed classes and pick me up in the short bus."

"Over my dead body."

"What if they made me do it whether or not you approve of the plan."

"What if another asteroid crashes into the earth?"

"I do have a lot of trouble understanding the plot of TV detective stories," Sophie says. "I forget who the characters are, and I ask Paul who are the good guys and who are the bad guys. It has never bothered me to ask Paul what's going on. And I get confused by books that have a lot of characters. I make diagrams connecting the characters — who is the mother and father and sisters and brothers of each character — and I look back at the diagram to remind myself of the relationship between characters. And I read the same book a couple of times so I know who everyone is, and the second time I read it I don't have to worry about forgetting them. Does that make me crazy or stupid? You don't have to answer."

"No one in the world could convince me you're either crazy or unintelligent."

"But what?"

"I didn't say 'but.'"

"But you thought it. Admit it."

"You'll never bully me into saying there was an unspoken 'but' in my mind."

———

The test results were delivered to the office of the Guidance Counselor at Sophie's high school. The school secretary called Sophie's father at work to arrange a time for him and Sophie to meet with Mr. Crenshaw.

Robert chose carefully the moment to tell Sophie's mother about the call from the guidance counselor's office. After dinner, in their bedroom, as Marjorie tidied up, Robert told her about the call.

"You know I can't stand going to these things where they diagnose the difficulty one of our children is having. You promised me you'd take care of this," Marjorie says pleadingly.

"Yes, I'll take care of it."

Robert, sitting on the bed next to Marjorie, tries to put his arm around her shoulder. Wiggling out of his embrace, she says, "Robert, I know you mean well, but I…."

"We went through it together, so why can't we be together in it now?" He tries to slide next to her, but she squirms away as if he's a stranger sitting next to her on a railway train.

"No, we each went through it on our own." Marjorie gets to her feet.

"It wasn't in your power, anybody's power, to change what happened," Robert, still sitting, says with a note of exhaustion in his voice, knowing how the conversation will end.

"I knew things weren't right. Anyone could have seen it. I'm grateful to you for going with Sophie to these things."

"I wish there were something I could do for you."

"Thank you. I mean that. Would you mind letting me rest here for a while on my own?"

———

Sophie and her father take the two seats in front of Mr. Crenshaw's gray metal desk. The office is cramped and overheated. Mr. Crenshaw, the Guidance Counselor, is a man who appears to be in his 60s. He is a large-framed man, wearing a crumpled tan suit. He has a head of thin, rusty brown hair that seems to have been left to grow wild like weeds in an abandoned garden.

"Thanks for coming in. I hope that you won't think this a wasted trip. I don't quite know what to tell you. I see, Sophie, that you haven't come to school for a while now, so something's not right, so we asked for testing to see if we can do better. The testing results are detailed, and I'll have to be honest, a bit esoteric for me. They show problems with organizing and sorting things, and difficulty with reading comprehension. I don't know what all of this means. You met with Dr. Nevin. What did she have to say?"

"She said I have trouble seeing the obvious." Sophie looks directly into Mr. Crenshaw's eyes as she speaks each word.

Mr. Crenshaw bellows with laughter. "Sorry, I have trouble seeing the obvious myself. I don't see why some people are paid a thousand times what other people are paid in the same organization. I just can't see it. In what way are they worth so much more than all the others? Is it because they're smarter or is it because they lack a conscience? I guess the answer's obvious, but I can't see it. I have the same problem you do, Sophie."

Sophie is amused, but she's not sure he's serious about what he's saying.

"I can put you in this class or that one because I think you might enjoy it more, but you might not, and then you'll have to come back to tell me and I'll try again, and so on until there are no more classes to try and hopefully by then you're 16 and can do what you please, though I hope you'll like school well enough to continue because there are interesting things in junior and senior year. They read *Moby Dick*, I love that book, I really do. And Stephen Crane, what a powerful book that *Red Badge of Courage* is, "the red sun pasted in the sky like a wafer," I love that line. But you're a girl and you may not be as interested in a war story as I am. You may like *Jane Eyre* better."

"*Jane Eyre*'s every school girl's favorite. I prefer *Gulliver's Travels* and *Brave New World*."

"If you like *Brave New World*, you probably also like *Nineteen Eighty-Four*."

"To tell you the truth, *Nineteen Eighty-Four* gave me nightmares for weeks — the brainwashing and the changing of history."

"That is one of the scariest books I can think of."

As Mr. Chrenshaw spoke, Sophie wondered if he was giving a performance or was speaking sincerely. It felt to her like the latter, and she felt deeply grateful to him for it.

When they returned home, Marjorie was pretending to be cleaning up the kitchen. Sophie went directly to her room. Marjorie asked Robert what had happened. He said, "Nothing, which is the best thing that could have happened." She understood without his having to explain.

———

Sophie did not return to school. She seldom left her room, even for meals. When everyone was out of the house at school or at work, she ate breakfast in the kitchen. In the early afternoon, she warmed up food her mother had made for dinner the previous night and had left for Sophie in the fridge. She had no appetite for anything else until breakfast the next morning. She lost quite a bit of weight. Robert spoke with their family doctor, talked with a close friend, and consulted a psychologist. He was able to get Sophie to begin therapy with a psychologist, but Sophie refused to continue after a few sessions saying she was bored because the therapist didn't say anything.

Paul brought her books from the library. She now liked short stories by Raymond Carver, Poe, and O. Henry, stories that were told so beautifully you didn't have to follow the plot, it was all in the way the words were used. She didn't miss her friends because she had come to realize she had no friends with whom she could talk honestly. She recognized this was liberating because she felt free of the need to take part in the never-ending performances in which girls her age participated — the theater of crushes, heartbreaks, and chatter about the sex lives of the teachers.

Robert found a private school that offered homeschooling. Surprising to Robert, and greatly relieving to Marjorie, Sophie seemed to want to prove she was an excellent student despite what she called the verdict handed down by Dr. Nevin.

Marjorie understood what it must be like for Sophie not to be able to leave her room. She had felt like doing the same when she was Sophie's age but hadn't had the nerve to do it. Marjorie hired Hillary, a college student, to come to the house and spend time with Sophie.

Hillary could be chirpy when talking with Marjorie, but she was unhurried and thoughtful when with Sophie alone. Sophie liked her. They sometimes played board games. "Life" was one of their favorites. They were amused by the fact the winner of the game of "Life" was the person who had the most money at the end of the game. In the spring, half a year after Hillary was hired, they began to go on walks for their "curative value, à la Thomas Mann," as Hillary called it. She stayed three or four hours at a time. Sophie accepted visits only from the members of her family and Hillary; she could not tolerate having more than one visitor at a time. If there were more, she would crawl under her bedcovers until only one person remained in her room.

As Sophie came to trust Hillary, there were many questions she had for her. One day, Sophie said to her, "I read about romances in books and see them in just about every movie ever made, but I don't have any desire to be in one. That's another thing I don't do like other people."

"Sophie, why would you want to be anyone else?"

"Because life would be so much easier if I were like everyone else, if I dreamt of having a boyfriend, of getting married, having a family. That would give me a direction in life. I just drift — one direction is as good as any other because none of them leads anywhere I want to go."

"You're young. Things happen at different paces for people. You may be impatient with your parents, and you hate them sometimes, but they are basically good, if limited, people so far as I can tell. Your father specially."

"You've fallen for him?"

"Not as someone to have a crush on, just as a father far better than mine."

———

Marjorie, a year and a half after hiring Hillary, asked her if she thought Sophie was ready to enroll at the local university. Hillary told her that she'd rather not get involved in making plans for Sophie. She was just there to be a friend or older sister to her. Marjorie was annoyed by Hillary's comment and only much later recognized the wisdom in it.

Sophie would talk with Robert and Paul and Hillary, but not with her mother. Marjorie tried not to feel hurt by it. Robert assured her that mothers and daughters are at odds during adolescence, but that was of little comfort to Marjorie. Sophie honestly didn't know why she couldn't bear her mother.

Months later, Sophie chose a time to talk with her mother. She could hear Marjorie downstairs in the kitchen a couple of hours after supper. When Sophie entered the kitchen, she startled her mother who was sitting by herself at the kitchen table as she sometimes did this time in the evening. Marjorie looked at her daughter as if Sophie had returned after a long absence that had changed her in ways that Marjorie was trying to fathom. Sophie sat at the table near her mother. She didn't quite know how to start, so she began at the heart of things. She told her mother that she had been accepted by the local branch of the state university and planned to begin in the fall. Marjorie, who felt she had not been a good mother to Sophie, didn't dare inquire about whether Sophie planned to live at home or in the dorms of the university, nor did she ask how Sophie felt about undertaking this plan. Instead, Marjorie asked if there was anything she could do to help Sophie with this plan. Sophie said she'd ask if she needed help with anything.

Robert was skeptical. The decision seemed unrealistic given Sophie's years of seclusion, but he tried to be encouraging when speaking to her.

Summer passed quickly. Sophie, now, after years of interring herself in her room, very much wanted to be able to leave home to attend the university. She decided to live in the dorms. There was much uncertainty disguised as punctiliousness as Sophie and her father packed the car with her bags and good-byes were said.

Once classes began at the university, Sophie recognized that she was no closer to being able to leave her room in the dormitory than she'd been able to leave her room at home. She dropped out just four days into the semester. Her roommates were kind to her and helped her pack and carry her things to her father's car.

It became increasingly clear to Sophie that if she didn't do something, she would never be able to leave her room at home. On her own, she obtained the application forms for the local junior college, and with as little fuss as possible, coordinated the bus schedule with her classes and commuted to the junior college. She took only one class which she attended twice weekly and passed the exams. No one in the family said a word about what she was doing. Hillary no longer came regularly to the house but dropped by now and again, not as a paid friend, but as an actual friend.

Two years later, Sophie left home to attend a small four-year college. She lived in the dorms where she found that the world had changed during her prolonged absence. Sophie didn't know what had made it possible for her to leave home now, but she was both pleased and frightened by the development.

———

Sophie felt self-conscious about being four or five years older than the other students in her year at college. It was difficult to feel at ease with other students. She imitated other girls, and in this way felt just like a college girl when she was with classmates and teachers. Sophie majored in English Literature in hopes of becoming a better writer, but she couldn't bring herself to show her teachers the stories she'd written.

In a philosophy course, Sophie read Isaiah Berlin's essay, "The Hedgehog and the Fox," in which Berlin says that the fox knows many things but the hedgehog knows one big thing. Sophie thought of herself as the hedgehog, but her one big thing felt like an illusion she had been keeping aloft most of her life.

The girl with whom Sophie shared a dormitory room during the first semester chose to room with someone else when she returned from Christmas vacation. The school asked Sophie to move to a single room. Ashamed, she moved her things late at night to avoid the scornful looks she anticipated.

During the summers she worked as a research assistant to Daniel Arnott, a professor of linguistics at MIT. He was impressed by her ability to quickly grasp his research. She hoped that his "one big thing" in his study of linguistics would become her one big thing too. When admitted to the MIT graduate program in linguistics, Sophie did her doctoral research with Dr. Arnott.

A simple one-room apartment in Cambridge with only enough space for her to cook, eat, read, and sleep, seemed to suit Sophie. When her parents and Paul visited a few weeks into the first semester, she said she was having trouble grasping her role in one of the research projects Dr. Arnott was conducting.

She was aware, as were her parents, that she made no mention of friends, much less a boyfriend. Sophie's parents supplemented her income in a spirit that felt kind and generous to her.

By the end of the first semester, Sophie began to feel that things were not nearly as grim as they had felt when her parents and Paul had visited. She felt she had found work to which she was willing to exert all her energy.

Sophie liked some of the members of the team in which she worked. The project on which Sophie was working was directed by Brad Cantrowitz, a 35-year-old unmarried man, with long dark curly hair and cowboy boots, who she found dashing. At the end of each day, she'd go to his office to hand in her scoring sheets and to chat for a bit. They occasionally had coffee together. There was an attraction between them, she thought, but she didn't want to make more of it than it was.

At the end of her second year in the doctoral program, Cantrowitz called for a team meeting to announce that he hadn't been able to secure grant funding to continue his research project. His voice was choked as he gave them the news, knowing that they would either have to find positions in one of the other linguistic laboratories at MIT or find a job at another university, both of which would be very difficult to do.

The shutdown of the project was crushing for Sophie. Only years later could she see that her romance with linguistics, and her romance with Brad Cantrowitz, had been daydreams quite disconnected from reality. Nonetheless, her time there had not been entirely wasted. She had never before felt part of a team or had a boyfriend or even wanted to have a boyfriend, even if it was an imaginary boyfriend.

———

On the closing of the lab, Sophie could not envision a future for herself. She felt as if she had been created in a way that did not prepare her to be an independent human being in the world. This was true, she thought, not simply because of her inability to see the obvious, but also because of her inability to be friends with anyone who was not being paid to be her friend.

Feeling desperately lonely, she longed to talk with someone, but she felt that she had no one with whom to talk other than her father. She felt uneasy about inviting him to meet her to talk, but one Sunday afternoon she decided to call the house hoping he'd pick up the phone, knowing that was likely because her mother hated to do it. Greatly relieved to hear his voice, she asked him to meet her at a café near her apartment, a half-hour drive for him.

Before her father arrived, Sophie carried her coffee and croissant to a table at the far end of the room. The café seemed to fancy itself a place for radical, enlightened university students with its overflowing, waist-high bags of coffee beans from every corner of the globe in the center of the room, and large black-and-white posters of Malcolm X, Che Guevara, and Huey Newton on the walls. The place seemed to be pandering to poseurs. Who was she to talk of poseurs? She, who was without a job or friends, or a boyfriend, or a place to work, and soon without a place she could afford to live?

Two women were sitting alone at small tables near the large windows. The street outside was holding onto its last bit of gray before giving way to black. One of the women — a large woman in her early 30s — was writing something on what appeared to be a test booklet taken from a stack of pale blue booklets she was grading. Perhaps she was a teaching assistant. The other woman was huddled over a book, looking terribly sad. They seemed to emit their own dull light.

Sophie couldn't say why she chose this café, a place that now seemed like a place for women without a man, women burying themselves in their work and their books. Sophie startled when her father pulled the chair out from under the opposite side of the small table.

"Dad, you're here. Sit down. Would you like some coffee or a pastry or a cookie or something?" He looked older than she remembered, the skin on his face looser, more rutted, the bags under his eyes more pronounced. She hadn't seen him for months, not since Christmas.

"Let me take a look at the menu. Maybe I'll have something. I'm glad you called. It's always good to talk with you."

"That's the problem. I don't know what I want to talk to you about. I don't know anything." Crying now, she brushed tears from her cheeks.

"You know a lot."

"What are you talking about?"

"You know what you like. What gives you pleasure and satisfaction."

"Like what?"

"I don't know this for sure, we haven't talked about it for a while, but I imagine you still love writing."

"I do, but I'm not a writer. I've never published a single word. I haven't shown anyone anything I've written since I showed you something ten or so years ago."

"A writer is someone who writes, not someone who publishes."

"But what is a writer who never shows anybody anything?"

"It's a writer writing. You'll be published when the stars are correctly aligned. There's a lot of chance to it. Your time will come. I'm sure of it."

"Honestly, I don't know how good my writing is. I have boxes full of things I've written."

"All of what you've written won't rot on the vine, it's all there waiting to be brought into this world."

"I don't know anything about the real world. The words of that psychologist who gave me the tests in high school are with me always. I lack common sense. I will always miss the train or wait for it forever because I don't have the actual train schedule, I just have the version I've written, which unfortunately has nothing to do with real trains. Now that I'm no longer a doctoral student, by the way, they've shut down my group at the university, so I don't have a job or a place where I'm studying. When I chose to study linguistics, I was hoping its use of the scientific method would ground me in something I could depend on so I wouldn't be inventing the world any longer. I would be able to just stand there and learn about it, the real world, not a world I've created."

"Sweetheart, your common sense isn't poor, it allows you to see things that no one else sees because they're all so sure they know everything."

"No, Dad, it really is terrible."

"When have you lacked common sense?"

She put her head in her hands. This was something she did as a child when she tried to gather herself. He remembered her as the little girl he adored. She wasn't pretty in a conventional sense, she was a little plump, a little plain, but she was beautiful in his eyes. When she talked about something important to her, her blue-gray eyes got big, as if all of her insides were coming out at you.

Sophie then looked up at her father. "It's strange. I lack common sense in everything I do, but it's hard to give an example ... I don't know if this is a good example, but a girl down the hall from me in our apartment building would knock on my door asking if I had time for a glass of wine or a cup of tea. I didn't know how to say "no" or to tell her I was tired so she should leave. I put up with her for a long time until one day I told her I didn't want her to come by so often because I had a lot of work to do and was facing a deadline on my dissertation. She went berserk saying that she had thought we were friends and had felt that I wasn't merely tolerating her. She stormed out. Every time we cross paths, which is pretty often, she gives me a scalding look. I should have ended things after the first time we talked, but I didn't know better."

"Sophie, do you have friends you can talk to about situations like this?"

"No, I don't have any friends. I know that sounds pathetic."

"Do you try to make friends?"

"I used to, but I've given up."

"When did you stop trying?"

Sophie exhaled deeply, searching her memory. "It's probably after my first year of college. You remember my roommate moved out of our dorm room after she got back from Christmas break. By the time I was in grad school a lot of people were either married or seeing someone for a long time. The girls who remained single were a group who were difficult to please. I thought of them as 'professional' at being on their own. They seemed no longer young. They were very clear about what they expected of friends and boyfriends. It was as if they were exclusive clubs that I would never be qualified to join."

"Those are clubs you're better off not joining."

"I'm just trying to tell you why I've given up on friendships. I know what you're thinking, that I've chickened out of friendships, chickened out of life."

"No, I'm not as judgmental as you are. I was just thinking that it takes luck to find people to be friends with. There are people out there who you just have to wait for, and you'll know when one of them comes along. But you can't do all of the waiting in your apartment."

"I thought you'd get around to blaming me for not having friends. I hide in my apartment, so it's no wonder I don't have friends. That's what you're saying, aren't you?"

"Slow down. What I had in mind is that there are other places to wait, like a school library or any other place that feels right to you."

"Dad, I can't tell what other people want. I can't tell if someone is just not interested in meeting a stranger. I have no idea how to read that feeling in their face and the way they talk. I get it wrong every time."

"These things are hard for everyone, but I understand that you're saying that, for you, these things are impossible. But it's also true that you're quite different from the person you were when you were unable to leave your room. You've come a long way from there."

"I sometimes think I haven't changed much from being who I was then. Lacking common sense makes it hard to hold a job and pay my expenses. That's something you and Mom have always been afraid of."

"That's not fair, Sophie. I've only wanted you to be happy with what you're doing."

"That word, 'happy.' I don't know what it means. I hear people talk about being happy with their jobs, their boyfriends, their lives. I don't know if they're talking about 'birthday-party-happy.' That's a feeling I've never experienced, even as a child. Feeling good is different, it's something I've felt sometimes. Maybe in a conversation, now and then, I feel good when I feel surprised by the smile on the other person's face. I feel it sometimes when reading when I feel, 'That's what good writing is: mysterious, clever, but not too clever,' a feeling that I'd like to write like that, and at the same time, not exactly like that. Sometimes I feel it would be a relief to give up writing, but that feeling of peace quickly decays into utter bleakness."

"I know, sweetie."

"No, you don't. You've never felt this way."

"I've never felt a lot of ways... ."

"Don't bullshit me."

"I know enough," he insists.

"I don't know that you do. I feel like there isn't a place on earth where I could fit in. Sometimes I wish I'd never been born. Have you ever felt that?"

"No, I haven't, but I've felt so humiliated I wished I were dead."

"When was that?" Sophie asks, not sure she wants to hear his reply.

"I've never talked about this with anyone but Mom."

"I don't want you to tell me anything you'd rather not say. Really, I don't."

"I want to tell you. It's hard to know where to start. For most of my childhood, I was a very insecure boy. I was a smart kid and did better than my friends at school, but when I got to college, there was much stiffer competition. I studied very hard, but it was difficult to keep up the pace I'd set for myself. Things came to a head in a biology course. The professor — I remember his name, Professor Koenigsberg — gave us an exam to take on our own on the honor system. I didn't have to cheat because I could have done well anyway, but I couldn't stop myself from looking up answers from the textbook. When the exams were graded and passed out to the class, Koenigsberg read out the grades he'd given and announced that only one student had a perfect score and I was the one who had done it. I felt certain he knew I'd cheated and was ridiculing me in front of the class. I was afraid the news of my cheating would spread like wildfire. There was no one I could talk to about what happened. I would have welcomed the end of everything. And that shame lasted a long time."

"I'm sorry, Dad."

"Sophie, I don't want you to feel sorry for me. I just want you to know you're not the first person to feel something like what you're feeling. But unlike me, you haven't done anything to feel ashamed of."

"Dad, I feel ashamed of everything. That's what I've been trying to tell you."

The two of them sat silently lost in their own thoughts for a few minutes.

It was now a little after 6:00. The large windows facing the street were a black screen with moving dots of light and pale reflections of the interior of the café.

"I'd better get home before the streets get icy. Let me drive you to your apartment."

"No, I'll walk. I like the cold air against my face as I think."

"Think and walk. Two birds with one rock."

"Yeah, two birds with one rock," he says.

———

That night, Sophie had a dream. When she awoke from it in the wee hours of the morning, she wrote down as much of it as she could remember and sent that page to her father the next day:

> On entering a big hall, I could see flickering light coming from a ramp just ahead. There was water flowing down the ramp in which there were schools of tiny iridescent fish. As I came closer, I saw that what appeared to be fish were words: English words, French words, German words, Greek words, words from every language. In this river of words were prefixes and suffixes that joined together to form longer words which splashed onto the walls of the ramp. As I stepped onto the ramp, words licked my feet and showered down from above like warm summer rain.

— UNDER SEIGE —

We heard rats scratching in the walls and ceiling of our bedroom. Mice don't make noises like the ones I was hearing. My wife, Francine, concurred. Life changed for me after hearing the sounds in the ceiling and walls.

The night I first heard the rats I checked the Yellow Pages for exterminators. I don't know why I decided on one that had a half-page illustration of a large rat being hit over the head by a hammer. The next morning, I called this company and arranged for a "technician" to meet me at the house that afternoon.

Our home — a modest, 1940s three-story house at the edge of the city — was now, for me, a different place from the one we'd purchased a year earlier. The house now seemed haunted, no longer a place where Francine and I could raise Dave, our three-and-a-half-year-old.

I grew up in a suburban town an hour north of Boston. I had seen mice in cartoons but was not aware that rats, animals five or ten times the size of mice, infested houses. I remember my mother telling me that my father had seen a mouse under the kitchen sink, a mouse that had slipped by our two cats who, I was told, patrolled the house in search of such creatures.

I vividly recall the day that rats began to figure largely in my imagination. Fears must have been brewing in me for some time, but when in high school I read the torture scene in *Nineteen Eighty-Four*, rats became terrifying. The State strapped a metal cage onto Winston Smith's head in which his face was separated by a metal door from starving rats. The door would be opened if Smith didn't renounce his false ideas. The night I read those pages, and for weeks afterward, I was unable to sleep. I've been terrified of rats ever since.

Any moving shadow on the floor sends a chill through me. I knew that rats are strong and can eat through sheet rock or lath and plaster, so there is no effective way to keep a room safe from them. It seems only natural to fear rats. They are the filthiest, most destructive creatures this world has ever known. They spread the Plague in the Middle Ages that killed millions of people. What is difficult for me to understand is why other people aren't as frightened of rats as I am.

When I first heard the rats in our house, I was 31, a year out of residency in internal medicine, working at a public health clinic. Francine is an intelligent, level-headed woman on whom I rely. She has her own fears, but her fears are different from — and fewer than — mine. For her, rats are revolting, but she isn't terrified of them. After we first heard the rats, Dave knew that something was wrong but relied on us to handle whatever it might be. He didn't hear them, so far as I know.

The technician arrived around 5:00 that Friday afternoon. Alan was a surprise. He was a man in his early 30s wearing a thick white shirt with the company logo imprinted on it along with a plastic name tag. Alan was polished in a salesman sort of way: he firmly shook my hand and looked me in the eye in an attempt to convey the feeling that he knew what he was doing, and that I could trust him.

Alan explained, "Extermination has a logic to it, which, if allowed to play out, will solve the problem of invasion by pests. The key is finding the entry point or points. So, let's start in the basement where the entry points are most often located." He saw the skeptical look on my face and said in a paternal way, "Don't worry, I've got this one."

Large plastic workbox in hand, Alan followed me down the cellar stairs. In addition to the furnace and water heater, the basement was filled with cardboard boxes we hadn't yet unpacked, boxes filled with Dave's baby clothes and toys, the parts of his crib, and other things we'd intended to use when we had a second child. Vertical water pipes were visible on the south wall of the largest of the three connecting rooms that made up the basement. Alan pulled from his belt a flashlight which he shone around the space the way a doctor might examine a child's tonsils. He pushed the boxes and paint cans aside as he looked for droppings at the foot of the walls.

He became interested in a portion of the basement immediately to the right of the water pipes. "Have a look at these. They're not shiny the way fresh droppings are, but they're not ancient either. This could be the place they entered before climbing up these pipes to the upper stories." Though I wanted to believe him, I was not convinced. The droppings were coated with dust.

"I'll place bait here in the path along the base of the wall I suspect they're traveling," he said. He filled several plastic trays with a granular mix and carefully laid them on the concrete floor leading to the pipes. As we left the basement, I locked the door so Dave couldn't get at the poison.

Alan and I then went to the kitchen where he examined the space under the sink. "Steel wool's needed around each of those pipes. Mice can get through quarter-inch spaces. They have whiskers like cats and their bodies are so malleable that they can get through almost any space no matter how small, even a space a quarter of an inch round. I'm talking mice now. Mice squeeze through holes, rats eat through walls."

Once upstairs, Alan took a look at the base of the walls of our second-floor bedroom and Dave's third-floor bedroom but found no droppings. He said he'd be back in three days to see what's happening. The noises persisted that night, another sleepless night for me. I spent the time in bed strategizing. I came to one conclusion. Alan was not capable of doing the job. I just didn't have confidence in him.

In fighting this battle, money was meaningless. I wondered what would happen if, when speaking to the next exterminator, I told him I'd pay him $20,000 if he could rid the house of rats in 48 hours and pay him nothing if he failed. I realized I was dealing in magic but the thought was vaguely comforting.

I looked at other advertisements in the Yellow Pages. The second company I chose had more subdued advertising but offered "guaranteed results." They scheduled a visit the following day. The technician came and inspected the house in a perfunctory way. He said the trays of poison already there would suffice and added some large rat traps.

I was living on very little sleep and in constant fear of the next sound in the walls, the sight of a rat racing across a room, a rat jumping onto our bed, a rat inside the bedding that would bite my feet. Living had become ahistorical. Yesterday, today, and tomorrow were interchangeable. Our eighth wedding anniversary occurred several days after we began hearing the rats, but it felt unreal, it held no significance. It didn't occur to either Francine or me to celebrate it. It was just another day. A wedding anniversary? What of it?

While this was happening, a friend, Stan Zeigler, was hospitalized for an illness that made it impossible for him to digest food. He was being fed intravenously. While visiting him, it occurred to me that Francine and I could sleep at his place until we'd rid our house of rats. I was fully aware that this line of thought was utterly self-centered. I was planning to do the equivalent of picking the pocket of a homeless man. I couldn't bring myself to ask this favor of Stan. It would be unseemly to profit from his misfortune. But during my third visit, after still more sleepless nights, I succumbed to the wish to ask him.

I had only known Stan for a few months. He was a psychologist, a few years older than I was. He'd been working at the clinic where I now worked for a year or so when I arrived. I genuinely liked him but really didn't know him very well. When I got up my nerve to ask him if we could sleep at his place, I explained the situation and urged him not to do anything that would be uncomfortable for him, particularly now when he had enough on his mind. "Of course, it's fine with me for you to use my place. But I haven't prepared for visitors or even cleaned and washed up the way I usually do."

I thanked him for his generosity and assured him that any un-tidiness would be welcome because straightening up would give me a small way of thanking him for allowing us to sleep there. Francine agreed that it was impossible for us to continue living at our house, but sleeping at Stan's apartment would not be easy since we would be returning home early each morning to prepare Dave for nursery school and ourselves for work.

That evening we packed clothes and toys in a duffel bag. Dave was at once puzzled as to why we were not sleeping at home and curious about the new place. We had not told Dave about the rats; instead, we invented a story about the need to move out of the house for a few nights because noisy work was being done next door that could only be done at night.

Stan's place was a small, sparsely furnished one-bedroom in a 1930s apartment building. There was a double bed but sleeping in Stan's bed felt like an imposition greater than what felt right to me. So, we slept in sleeping bags on the living room floor. I slept better than I had in the eight days since the noise in the walls had begun.

During the days that followed, we each went to work or school as usual, but there was nothing usual about it. We drove home from Stan's in the early morning, brushed our teeth, put on clean clothes, and managed to get to the breakfast table where none of us had much of an appetite. At the end of the workday Francine and I returned home, bid good night to the au pair, and prepared dinner. Dinner, too, felt like a charade in which we were imitating living the life we had once lived. After dinner, we watched TV to pass the time. I turned the volume up loud to drown out the possible sound of rats. Around 9:00 we loaded the car, drove to Stan's, and lugged the toys and food up to Stan's second-floor walk-up apartment. I don't know why we bothered bringing food we never ate. We put on our pajamas, read bedtime stories, and then climbed into our sleeping bags only to be met by the unforgiving solidity of the floorboards. Each night we spent on the floor felt more difficult, more impersonal, and more uncomfortable than the previous night.

At home, when I allowed myself to check to see if I could hear the sound made by the rats, it was discouraging to find that the noise seemed to have increased from what it had been when I first heard it.

I hired a third pest control man with little hope that he would know anything more than the first two. Vernon didn't wear a uniform. He didn't work for a company, he was the company. He told me that his principal tool was his "animal instinct," his instinct about animals' behavior which he acquired while growing up in rural Kentucky. I told him about the rats in our ceiling and walls. He asked if we'd found any droppings. I said we'd found some dried droppings at the beginning, but there were no new ones.

He checked the basement and kitchen and then asked, "How do I get out on the roof?" The second exterminator had inspected the roof but had found nothing suspicious. As we walked up to the third floor, Vernon said he thought it might be roof rats. "There's a fair number of them round here." He climbed through a third-floor window onto a flat, gravel-topped area of roofing. I climbed out onto the roof after him. Looking around for half a minute, he leaned down and picked up some splinters of red-painted wood that came off the shingles on the back of the house.

He poked under the eave and said, "This here's your problem. You got a hole under here, most likely where they're gettin' in." He motioned to me to stick my hand under the eave. I didn't like poking my hand into a rat hole. I could feel a hole about the size of a cantaloupe. I asked Vernon what he'd suggest doing. "Might as well nail it shut. You got some wood and nails." I said I'd run and get them from the basement. "Don't rush yourself, it's nice out here."

Vernon nailed a six-by-nine-inch board over the hole and said, "We'll know more in the morning." After he left, I pounded more nails into the board covering the hole.

I felt relieved to have Vernon on the case. I didn't dare hope that plugging the hole was the solution to the problem, but I slept more soundly that night at Stan's.

Anxious to know whether we had, in fact, plugged the entry point, I awoke early and drove home before Francine and Dave woke up. I climbed out onto the roof to find that the board had been wrenched off the hole under the eave. The nails were bent on the board that lay on the gravel-topped section of the roof. I was frightened by the strength of the rats. If they were able to tear off the board, they had the strength to defeat any effort I might make to block their entrance to the house. The house was theirs.

I re-nailed the board over the hole and used twice the number of nails that had been used the previous day. I then brought up from the basement three of the cinder blocks that I'd found under the deck when we moved in. I placed two of the cinder blocks as close as I could to the board nailed over the hole and I placed the other one against the adjacent shingles.

The next morning when I checked the board and cinderblocks, there was no indication the cinder blocks had been moved. I called Vernon and told him about this development. We arranged a time to meet at the house at the end of the day. Once the two of us were out on the roof, he looked at the barricade I'd built and said, "We're not dealing with rats. Let's find out what we got here. Spread some flour around out here and we'll see what sort of creature this is." I did as he instructed, probably using a greater quantity of flour than he had in mind. There was nothing more to do but wait till the next morning, which came very slowly. I was worn out and tired of sleeping on Stan's floor.

When morning arrived, I drove back home just before dawn and found paw prints all over the flat area of the roof where the hole was located. Not only was that part of the roof covered with paw prints, but there was a path of prints over the top of the roof to the other side. After I climbed back into the house, I walked into Dave's bedroom on the other side of the house. On the two double-hung windows next to Dave's bed there were ten or twelve paw prints that made me smile, which was something I could not remember having done since the invasion of the house began. It looked like a cartoon animal had stood on its hind legs pushing its face against the windowpanes trying to see what's happening inside. But the faint comedic quality of the paw prints almost immediately gave way to the disgust I felt when I imagined a desperate animal only a few inches from Dave's head.

I couldn't identify the paw prints, so I had to wait until Vernon came around at the end of the day. On taking one look at the windows, he said, "You got raccoons." I asked if that was good or bad. He said, "It's bad only 'cause there's a state law saying you're not 'lowed to kill 'em. You can kill 'em in Kentucky. I can never understand why you can't kill 'em here, but they got a law against it. What you got here is a mother raccoon going out at night through the hole under the eave and bringing back food for the babies born inside the house. You're now dealing with a mother separated from her babies. Any mother animal goes crazy when that happens."

I asked him what our options were. He said, "We could uncover the hole at night — probably around nine or ten — and watch from the window that lets out onto the roof. If we're lucky, the mother will take the babies with her when she goes out for food. After they're all out of the house, we could nail the hole shut so they can't get back in. Now, that depends on her taking the younguns with her."

Doubtful that this plan would work, I asked if there were other options. "You can try 'Have-a-heart' traps." He said they're metal cages inside of which you put a can of food on a lever. The door slams shut behind the animal when it touches the food on the lever. You notify the city's animal control people, and they'll tell you where to bring the animal you've caught in the trap. He told me the name of the company that sells these traps.

Knowing that we were dealing with raccoons, not rats, was greatly relieving to me, but the idea of a mother raccoon willing to try anything to reach her babies was also frightening to imagine. Vernon warned me that the babies would soon be hungry and crying for their mother. The crying began that night and was too loud for us to sleep at home. By now I realized that the noises we had heard in the walls and roof of the bedroom were made by the baby raccoons as they played. They were probably batting something around, perhaps small blocks of wood left behind by carpenters in the space between the second and third floors and in the space between the interior and exterior walls of the house.

The "Have-a-Heart" trap was delivered to the house. It's a big contraption. I carried it to the back porch and set it up. I gently placed on the lever the can of cat food I'd bought at the supermarket. On coming home the next morning, I found the trap had not been sprung, but the can of cat food I'd placed on the lever was gone. I felt as if I were playing chess with an opponent far better than I was. I reset the trap. The can of cat food was not touched that night. I keep the trap stocked with fresh cat food every night after that.

In talking with Vernon in the wake of these failures, he mentioned a third option. "I could bring my rifle and shoot the mother raccoon when she returns from gathering food. She'll be here on the roof with food. I know that for a fact." I thanked him but said it seemed too dangerous. Someone in the house across the way could get shot by a stray bullet. But I was touched by Vernon's offer.

A day or two later, I climbed out onto the roof as I did each morning. Nothing had changed there, nor was there anything new outside the windows of Dave's bedroom. But while dressing on the second floor, I noticed that the narrow deck outside a second-floor window was cluttered with broken shingles. I climbed out of the window that opens onto that deck and found, on looking up, that the top row of a dozen or so shingles had been torn off. The mother raccoon must have leaned over the edge of the roof to try to make a new entrance for herself by prying off the upper row of shingles.

When Vernon came to the house around 6:00 in the evening, I asked where we go from here. He said, "What we do with raccoons where I grew up is put out cat food laced with arsenic. But you may have a problem with that." I was desperate and told him, "I have no problem at all with that. Where do you get arsenic?"

"I don't know, maybe you could get it at a pharmacy. In Kentucky, farmers use arsenic to kill whatever's eatin' their chickens or their crops."

Later that day, I walked to the local pharmacy where they knew me and asked if they sold arsenic. The woman at the cash register called back to the pharmacist asking if they carried arsenic.

The pharmacist called back saying, "I'm not a character in an Agatha Christie play." He chuckled to himself and then yelled back, "It's possible one of the old drugstores downtown has some in their basement." When I phoned one of these old pharmacies asking if they still stocked arsenic, the man answering the phone hung up on me, probably thinking it was a prank call.

I called agricultural supply houses in the Valley. After being told by several supply houses that they'd stopped selling arsenic, I reached a woman who didn't talk to me as if I were a lunatic. She said I'd need a medical license to buy it. When I told her I was a licensed physician, she gave me the phone number of an agricultural pharmaceutical supply house. I called and asked if they stocked arsenic pentoxide (by now I was fluent in arsenic terminology). The woman asked me how much I'd like to buy. I had no idea how much I needed. The woman was kind enough to give me a clue by saying that it comes in eighths of a pound. I ordered a quarter pound, which she said she'd set aside for me.

I found someone to cover for me at the clinic for three or four hours. While driving to the pharmaceutical supply house, I felt like a spy or an assassin. I had told no one, not even Francine, about my plan to use arsenic to poison the mother raccoon which would leave the babies on their own to starve to death. I knew I was breaking the law, not only state law, but laws of ethics, but I couldn't stop myself from going ahead with the plan. While driving to the neighboring town, I imagined that the business would be located on a dirt street at the very edge of town where shady dealings are conducted like the ones I'd seen on television. I was surprised to find that the supply house had a parking lot no different from other ordinary small businesses.

On entering the building, I found myself in a large room decorated with stand-up cardboard photographs of large John Deere tractors and other agricultural equipment in shades of shiny green, yellow, and red. At the far end of the room on the right, a woman in her 50s was standing behind a counter. She looked at me with a welcoming smile. When I told her my name, I sounded to myself like a grade school child collecting something at the drug store his mother had asked him to pick up.

The woman said, "Yes, I have that for you. I need to have you show me your medical license." I gave her the license, which she photocopied.

A man in his early 20s, who I took to be a member of the family that owned the business, retrieved the bottle that had been set aside. The arsenic was in a brown, semi-transparent glass bottle of the sort you'd expect to find at a pharmacy in early twentieth-century America. The thought occurred to me to pay in cash in order not to leave a paper trail.

I stopped at a supermarket on the way home to buy a can of cat food. I felt strange buying the cat food, not to feed an animal, but to kill one.

On returning home, I climbed to the third floor of the house. No one was home. I stopped and considered what I was doing. I hesitated to put a can of cat food laced with arsenic out on the roof. I didn't want to kill the neighbor's cat who might eat the poisoned food if the mother raccoon were to knock the can down into the garden below. I walked down to the basement and found a four-foot board among the wood I had accumulated for small carpentry jobs. I brought it, along with a hammer and nails, up to the third floor.

I had gathered there a bowl, spoon, and can opener along with the bottle of arsenic and the can of cat food — a veritable assassin's workshop. I opened the can, dumped the cat food into the bowl, and then nailed the base of the empty can to the board. How much arsenic does it take to kill a raccoon? They don't teach you that in medical school. I had a queasy feeling in my stomach and tried not to think about what I was doing. I mixed a couple of tablespoons of the white arsenic powder in with the cat food. I spooned the mixture back into the can now nailed to the board.

I leaned out of the window and placed the board and poison-filled can of cat food on the flat portion of the roof. I climbed out onto the roof and positioned the plank closer to the boarded-up hole under the eave. I asked myself again if I really wanted to do this. My answer was still "yes." I knew I wasn't going to let the mother back in the house and that I was torturing her by keeping her separate from her babies. I tried to assure myself that the neighbor's cat doesn't climb three stories to lie in the sun on our roof. It was now almost three weeks since we'd been sleeping on the floor of Stan's apartment. Only one family could occupy the house — the family of raccoons or our family. The work of killing the raccoons was mine alone. I could not ask Francine to take part in it. This is a man's job, I said to myself.

The next morning, on returning to the house, I saw that the can of cat food on the roof had been emptied. The mother never returned and the babies' crying became more desperate, until one night it stopped altogether. We then moved back into our house.

Vernon had cautioned me that the bodies of the dead baby raccoons would create a stench that would make it impossible for us to live in the house for at least a month, probably two. And there would be swarms of flies bloated by having fed on the babies' dead bodies. He said he could open up the floor of the third story to try to remove the dead babies, but it would be very difficult to locate them because it's almost impossible to determine precisely where the odor is coming from.

With the death of the babies, the curse of the flies began. On the first day, I swept up many hundred, perhaps a thousand, dead flies from the basement and the three floors above. Many more, still alive, flew lazily around the house. Each day there were fewer flies both living and dead. And there was no odor. Vernon said he'd never before seen the death of raccoons inside the walls of a house not leave a terrible stench. He said I was lucky, which seemed a strange word to use in the light of all that had happened.

— A MORNING WITH MARIA KODAMA —

It was a brisk spring morning, the 25th of September, 2007. The three of us were waiting in front of a tall black door at the end of an 8-foot-high stone wall. The building behind was an imposing residence in the fashionable Recoleta District of Buenos Aires. I could see only its upper stories. In the wall of the house immediately to the right of this one, a bronze plaque read:

> *Jorge Luis Borges resided here in 1939*
> *when he wrote* The Circular Ruins.

It seems to me that no writer since Borges, or before him, is free of Borges' influence. Borges' *ficciones* constitute a literary genre in which the center of the universe is at every place in the universe; in which all humans are one human, and each human is all humans; in which every story is realistic save one fantastical element, which makes reality fantastical and the fantastical real; in which the author creates the literary work, and the literary work creates the author; in which each reader writes the story he is reading, and the story writes the reader; in which every task is labyrinthine, and the perfect labyrinth is a straight line; in which any given moment is all of time, and all of time is in any given moment.

David Rosenfeld invited my wife, Sandra, and me to join him in visiting Maria Kodama, Borges' widow. It was not clear to me how he arranged this meeting. He said he knew people who knew her, but she did not know him.

We were told to arrive at ten minutes to 10:00, which led me to think that we would have ten minutes with Maria Kodama. A short, thick woman, with graying hair pulled back tightly in a bun, opened the door to the street at a little after ten. She gave us a dutiful smile. Seeming to know who we were, or not caring who we were, she led us along a brick path that bisected the formal garden at the front door of the house.

We climbed three stairs to the large open front door from which poured sallow yellow light. On entering the house and walking down a short, dimly lit hallway, a large living room opened to our left, two steps down from where we were standing. The room was elegant — with its soaring, eighteen-foot ceilings, ornate crown molding, brass handles, and escutcheons — but it was also a shambles, not the shambles of an abandoned or derelict building, but the shambles of a theater stage strewn with props and tools, perhaps what remained of a stage set of a play that had had its run, or the beginnings of a stage set for a play about to open. Framed paintings of dark landscapes and ancient ruins leaned against two of the walls. The windows were mottled with dust and streaks of grease.

The three of us stood awkwardly with the woman who let us in. She and David conversed in Spanish in a strained way. As we waited, I made the mistake of trying to talk with the woman who let us in, who looked to be in her early sixties. I told her that my tie to my older son is deeply rooted in our shared love of Borges. She didn't seem to understand. I felt foolish for expecting this woman to be bilingual and able to respond to what I'd said.

It was now a quarter past 10:00. We heard the clinking and scraping of a key trying to find the right angle for turning a lock; a few seconds later, we watched a woman entering the room from the hallway, saying first in Spanish, then in English, that she was sorry to be late and hoped we hadn't been waiting long. Maria Kodama was an exotic-looking woman. What was most striking on first seeing her was the stripe of white at the front edge of her pitch-black hair, a lock of which now and again slipped forward, covering the left side of her face. She appeared to be in her mid- to late-fifties. Her face was a delicate play of her father's Japanese ancestry and her mother's European ancestry, a lineage Borges had mentioned in his essay on his excursion to Japan.

After we introduced ourselves, Maria Kodama, to my surprise, asked if we would like to have her show us the house. I was confused by the fact that she asked that question in a way that left open the possibility that we would say, "No, we're too busy to see it."

We followed her up a flight of worn wooden stairs, past a casement window on the first landing, which brought to mind the casement windows in the library where Borges worked as a young man. Due to his poor eyesight, he cut his forehead on one of these casement windows left open after having been painted earlier in the day. He sank into a febrile coma and was hospitalized for a dozen days. On waking, what was of most importance to Borges was demonstrating for himself that he could still write.

Borges decided that the only true test of his ability to write would be to compose in a genre in which he had tried to write but had never succeeded: the genre of the short story. What he wrote was "Pierre Menard, Author of the Quixote," the first of his *ficciones*, a genre of fantastical literature that is uniquely Borges. In "Pierre Menard," which is set in the early 20th century, Menard set himself the task of writing *Don Quixote* — not an imitation of it or a modern-day version of it, but the *Quixote* itself. A passage from Menard's *Quixote* and a passage from Cervantes' *Quixote* are identical on the page of Borges' text, word for word, comma for comma.

But Borges finds Menard's *Quixote* "almost infinitely richer" than Cervantes'. Menard's is more subtle, more philosophically sophisticated. Of course, Cervantes' *Quixote* is devoid of the banal practice of adding local color because his readers were familiar with the customs and practices of 17th-century Spain, but for Menard to desist from adding local color is an act of genius, a genius so vast that one can hear in Shakespeare the influence of Menard.

At the top of the staircase to our right was a room that housed most of Borges' books, which included his father's books, all of which were written in English, his father's first language. Borges wrote that he grew up in his father's library. As a boy, Borges thought that the language in which he spoke with his father and his British grandmother was a literary form of Spanish, while the language he spoke with his mother and the servants was an everyday form of Spanish. The room we'd just entered was overflowing with books — books askew leaning against one another on shelves, books in piles on tables and chairs and the floor, a small stack on a window ledge. A faint scent of vanilla filled the room, reminiscent of the scent of books in the underground levels of a library.

Maria asked me if I would like to hold one of the books. I was startled by her question because it seemed to me that Borges' books should not be damaged by the oils of one's hands. I told her I would like that very much. She asked if there was one in particular I would like to hold.

By chance, on a shelf just above the one in front of me was the faded spine of Borges' father's English translation of *Don Quixote*. Borges had read this book before reading *Don Quixote* in Spanish. On first reading the book in Spanish, it seemed like a poor translation. The sensation of the heft of the book in my hands felt as if I were shaking hands with Borges as if the weight of the book were the firmness of the grasp of his handshake. I felt the difference, the asymmetry, of the experience of the soft hand of a blind man in the grip of that of a man with sight.

After I returned the book to its place, Maria led us down the windowless hallway to the last door on the right in which there was a narrow single bed resembling an army cot, placed sternly in the far corner of the room, a window just past the foot of the bed. Against the wall, opposed to the foot of the bed, was a modest bookcase of four shelves filled with books. An austere wooden chair stood next to the head of the bed; across the room stood a plain dresser of dark wood.

There were two photographs on the walls of the room, one above the bed, the other above the dresser. Both were photographs of Maria and Borges, one taken in what looked like a Paris café; the other outdoors, possibly at a ranch in the south of Uruguay, where as a boy, Borges spent summers, and where one of the *ficciones*, "Funes the Memorious," is set.

The bookshelf at the foot of the bed, Maria told us, was filled with Borges' favorite books, which he wanted close to him when he slept. Maria, speaking softly as if in a sacred place, said that she was very young when she met Borges at a seminar on Norse literature that Borges was conducting at the National Library. He had been appointed Director of the National Library after the fall of Peron. In a poem, he speaks of the irony of being given 800,000 books at the same time that his eyesight completely failed him.

Maria explained to us, haltingly, that she spent most of her time reading works in ancient languages — Greek, Latin, Norse, and Icelandic. I had read that on Borges' tombstone in Geneva, there are engraved images of Norse gods and goddesses from mythic Norse love stories in which Borges and Maria imagined themselves as the protagonists.

—

We climbed the stairs to the third floor of the house and then outside to the roof garden. It was open on all four sides, each side looking down on the street and the gardens of neighboring houses and up to the bright morning sky. Maria, speaking in hushed tones, as if telling a secret, directed our attention to the garden of the house next door, the house with the plaque in its front wall.

The garden was made up of a large jacaranda with violet blooms on several branches, standing off-center among dark green shrubs. There was a tall brick wall thick with vines at the far end. There was a serenity about the place.

Maria told us, "I knew, everyone knew, that Borges lived in the house next to the one we're in when he wrote 'The Circular Ruins.' Borges and I didn't meet until much later. After Borges died, I followed the real estate section of the newspaper, hoping that the house next door would come up for sale so I might see the garden where Borges wrote that story.

"When the house we're in did eventually come up for sale, I called the agent selling this house and pretended that I was interested in buying it. When the agent and I arrived here, I told her that I could not lie to her. I was interested to see this house, not to buy it, but with the hope that I might be able to look into the garden of the house where Borges wrote 'The Circular Ruins.'

"The agent told me that from the moment she received my phone call, she knew who I was and why I wanted to see the house. She said we had met at a gathering soon after Borges died. I have very little memory of that period and did not recall meeting her. The agent said she was happy to show me the roof garden of this house from which I could see the garden next door.

"We were up here in this rooftop garden when the agent asked if I would like to buy this house. I was startled by the question. I told her that I had no money, and it was out of the question for me to buy it. I explained that I lived in a small apartment and supported myself through the writing I do. She persisted and asked me what I could pay for the house. I told her again that I had no money; I couldn't pay anything. She pressed me to tell her what I would be able to pay, however little. I told her the very small amount I could pay for it.

"She explained to me that the owner of this house was a man who loves Borges' writing and bought the house because it is next door to the one where Borges once lived. The realtor said that she would tell the owner of the house what I was able to pay.

"The next day, she called me to say that the owner of the house would be pleased to sell it to me for the small amount I was able to pay. I have not met him because he was not at the closing. I have never lived in this house. I made it the home for the Borges Foundation and for his library and manuscripts. I am shy about the story I just told you. You can understand why."

I wondered why she felt shy about what she'd told us. Perhaps because she felt that it wasn't really she who'd bought the house, for she was a mere veil worn by Borges. She was an illusion. She did not exist — not even for us, the people with whom she was talking in a way that seemed personal. In going to meet her that day, I hadn't been anticipating meeting Maria Kodama, I had anticipated meeting Borges' widow. Can I honestly say, even now, that she is, for me, a person in her own right, a person other than Borges' widow?

Maria, after showing us the house, asked if we had time to have a cup of coffee with her at a nearby café. Finding that the café was not yet open, she suggested we take a taxi across town to a café owned by a friend. During the cab ride, Maria and I were seated next to one another. While sitting there, I recalled that when Perón was elected president, Borges was working in a small branch of the public library on the outskirts of Buenos Aires. He was also at the time a well-regarded essayist who wrote for a Sunday Buenos Aires newspaper. In response to Borges' stance against him, Perón, to humiliate Borges, briefly imprisoned Borges' mother and sister, removed Borges from his job as a librarian, and appointed him to the job of chicken inspector.

I'd read that Borges had not given public lectures before he lost his job at the library because of his severe anxiety about public speaking. He had listened in shame from the back row of auditoriums while a friend read the lecture Borges had written. After losing his job at the library, he had to find another way to support himself.

I hesitated to ask Maria something personal about Borges, but I told Maria that I did not understand how Borges managed to transform himself after the rise of Peron into the relaxed, witty public speaker whom I heard on the recordings of the Norton Lectures that Borges delivered in 1967. He seemed to be enjoying himself as he spoke, reciting from memory long passages of poetry. I said that his voice sounded as if he were talking comfortably with his father and grandmother.

Maria told me that Borges had a stutter from the time he was a young boy and was terrified that when he took the podium to lecture, he wouldn't be able to utter a word. After losing his job at the library, Borges had no source of income other than talks he was invited to give. It was no longer an option for him to have someone read his lectures, for he knew he would not continue to be invited to give talks if he did not deliver them himself. "For a long time, Borges was only able to deliver lectures after he drank pastis, but he felt ashamed of this, and felt physically ill after the lecture. Borges asked me if I thought it was all right for him to drink before he gave his lectures. I told him he should drink if that's what he wanted to do."

She explained that just before Borges was to deliver his public lectures, he would deliver the whole lecture to her in private and then drink pastis before delivering the lecture to his audience. This went on for a long time.

"One evening before a lecture, he told me that he wouldn't need to drink alcohol this time because there would be only one person in the audience that night, and that would be me, and he knew he could give the lecture for me because he had just done so. From that night on, he was able not only to give the lecture without drinking beforehand, he could also laugh and let his mind go where it would."

The café in the Boca District that Maria had in mind for us was not yet open when we arrived, but after Maria pressed the doorbell, a tall man walked down the dark passageway to the gate. Seeming at first annoyed by intruders, on recognizing Maria a sincere smile crossed the man's face. He was a handsome man of about 40, with long, wavy dark hair, dressed in black pants and a white shirt under a white apron. On unlocking the gate and swinging it open, introductions were made. Luis invited us to follow him down the dark passageway under a dreary house. We reached a sunlit, brick patio at the rear. Metal tables with folded legs leaned against the wall to our right.

Luis unfolded a metal table and four chairs and set the table with cloth napkins and silverware. Once we were seated, Maria leaned toward my wife, Sandra, saying something to her I couldn't hear. I found myself staring at Maria's face, which was half-covered by a tress of hair. The most powerful feature of her face was her dark brown eyes, which had the slightest hint of green to them. She seemed at first to be a woman whose life had already been lived, but as I continued to steal glances at her, I saw a glint of something more.

Maria glanced across the table at me. I feared that she caught me looking at her. Not wanting to embarrass me, she turned back to Sandra. I heard her saying something about a film, but I missed both the name of the film and the reason for its having come to Maria's mind.

Turning to David and me, Maria said, "We were talking about a film in which a man and woman fall in love. The man knows the woman's... ." Maria turned to David for help finding the English word she was looking for, but before David could answer, she said, "He knows every detail of her life. He knows the woman's past, present, and even her future — he knows everything there is to know about her, more than she knows about herself.

"One day, she passes a shop and sees in the window a pair of red shoes that are at once garish and adventurous. She impulsively buys them and goes dancing in them. The man who knows every detail of her life does not know about this. This is such an important thing about people."

Maria paused and apologized to Sandra and me for her terrible English. I thought that at this moment it was not her English that failed her; it was the difficulty of putting into words what she felt while watching this film and the way in which that feeling had stayed with her. Maria continued, "We need .... at any rate, I need to have things that the people I love don't know about me. I am at my core a recluse. The things that the ones we love don't know about us are the things we have to give them, the things they will never know. That is our bank ... no ... what is the word ... our treasure ... that's right, but . . . what is the word?"

She turned to David. He replied, "Gifts."

"Yes, those are the gifts we have for those we love: what they will not ever know about us."

It felt to me that Maria, in speaking of her understanding of the film, was putting into words — with disarming honesty — an aspect of her relationship with Borges. The gift she and Borges gave to one another was the gift of what each kept from the other.

Maria refused Borges' many proposals of marriage. It was only when they were in Switzerland, a month before he died, that Maria agreed to marry Borges so that upon his death she would hold sole ownership of his published and unpublished literary work and would protect them from his sister and other people whom Borges did not trust.

I did not ask the question in my mind: Why was Maria, a very private person, meeting with the three of us? I wondered if she felt responsible, as owner and executor of Borges' literary works, to be Borges' ambassador to the world. That morning, was I the burden she was carrying for him or was there something in this that Maria was doing for herself?

Footsteps — high heels unsteady on the bricks — closed in on us. The calm that had settled upon the four of us as we'd talked was unsettled. A woman in her mid-fifties, expensively dressed — both wrists gleaming with gold and silver bracelets, a delicate bronze triangular piece hanging from her neck, and large silver hoops dangling from her ears — greeted Maria as if she and Maria were close friends. Maria looked uncomfortable, a bit embarrassed by the noise this woman, Estela, was making.

Estela seemed to exude sympathy for Maria, sympathy for her obligation to entertain garish Americans, and I suspect, beneath her airs, annoyance that she was not invited to join us. Maria retained her composure. There was something unwavering in Maria: her dedication to representing Borges' literary estate, though, I think, was not something Maria would have chosen for herself. Agreeing to marry Borges to ensure the protection of his work was an act of self-sacrifice and love. She had no interest in the business of copyrights and foundations, but she was willing to assure Borges she would fulfill that function so he could die knowing his legacy was in safe hands. But the self-sacrifice to which she had committed herself could have easily become a form of suicide if she were not able to manage it, if she were not able to put it in a place separated from the place where she lived her own life, her private life, in her small apartment, where she protected her secrets and wrote and read Greek, Latin, Icelandic, and Norse literature.

Estela sat at a table close by, pretending not to be eavesdropping as she sipped her espresso. We thanked Maria for taking the time to meet with us. She told us there were some books in Spanish written about Borges by friends and acquaintances waiting for us at the house where we met her.

When we pressed the doorbell of the house, it felt to me that we were returning to the place where we began, but something had changed. We waited as the woman we dealt with earlier collected the books that were written in Spanish — the usual set of books for guests, I imagined. She handed the books to David and me, and wished us well in the phrases of English she knew, now daring to speak a few words in English. The books had a solidity to them that felt so different from the gift I had received that morning. I had seen in Maria much that I could not have imagined, and as importantly, came to see differently all that I did not know about her and Borges. I was reminded of a man I once saw on the paved path of the Emperor's Summer Palace in Beijing. He painted the characters of an ancient Chinese poem on the sidewalk, using a long-handled brush that he dipped in an old coffee can filled with water. The characters he drew in columns on the sidewalk evaporated one after the other in the warmth of the sun as he drew the succeeding characters.

—

On March 26, 2023, Maria Kodama died without leaving a will, which left the rights to Borges' works unclear. On June 27, a civil court in Buenos Aires ruled that Maria Kodama's nieces and nephews are the rightful owners and managers of Borges' estate.

About Thomas Ogden

Thomas Ogden, MD, published his internationally acclaimed novel, *The Parts Left Out*, in 2014. He has subsequently published two novels: *The Hands of Gravity and Chance* and *This Will Do* … These novels, along with thirteen books of psychoanalytic essays and literary criticism, have been published in more than twenty-five languages. He practices psychoanalysis in San Francisco where he teaches both psychoanalysis and creative writing.

About Sphinx & Sul Books

Sphinx is the fiction imprint of Sul Books.

Born from a collaboration of two long-time independent esoteric publishers, and named to honor the Suleviae — the sisterhood of goddesses revered at springs throughout Europe — Sul Books is dedicated to publishing works that manifest aspects of the sacred sight that heals what humans have harmed.

As with the thrice-fold kinship of the Suleviae goddesses, Sul Books combines the publishing strength of three resilient imprints: Sphinx Books, RITONA, and Gods&Radicals Press. Arising from these continuing legacies comes a fourth imprint, Sul Books, committed to stand-out works of powerful transformation.

Each of our imprints is guided by a commitment to pluralism, dissent, and the autonomy of humans, with a core focus on the importance of indigenous, animist, and non-industrial ways of being in the world.

Find out more at SULBOOKS.COM